MW00831849

Copyright to Christopher M Struck, 2017

All Rights Reserved.

Twitter: @struck_chris • Instagram: @struck_chrism

struckchris.com

Cover by Carla Johnson

CarlaJohnson.me

This book is dedicated to all those people that
believed in me.
My dads, mom, brothers, grandmas, family.
My friends.
My colleagues.
The English teachers who did.
And, finally the English teachers who didn't.

Without the people who said give up, I would not
have put in the work to prove you wrong. The people
who said go for it, I've been working
to prove you right.

I thank you all.

Special thanks to Nils Hanson for the enlightening
discussions and sharing his story. Also, special thanks
to Ruth-Anne Bender for the enlightening discussions
and sharing her stories.

What follows is a love letter to the world, the United
States of America, and to New York. Thank you.

Kennig and Gold

Christopher M Struck's
Modern American Tragedy

Nils,

You have been an inspiration to a young man who often finds the need to learn from the great and successful what it takes to live and love. There has been nothing greater than your friendship and kindness. You have taught me to believe in something stronger and bigger than the individual. Thank you so much and here's to many more notches on the belt. Cheers

Your friend,
Chris Struck

C. M. Struck's ♦

A Good Thing
Chapter 1

A cold day. That fifth of April.

I remember it like it was yesterday. I know that is cheesy to say, but I do. It's as much a curse as it is a blessing. I wish I knew then what I know now. One of life's simplest truths. You know, and maybe you don't, but you should. You can never have enough of a good thing when you can get it, because there is no guarantee that it will remain.

I was sitting, alone, at a table on the street with a view of the boulevard and a row of hyacinths and day lilies that stretched in the sun along the side of the road. An elm cast its shade across the table before me, but my glasses and hat hid my eyes. I tightened my jacket to mid-chest and stared deep into the pages of my book with little care as to what, when, or why anything happened around me.

I turned the page.

A gust of wind. It was then that she sat down. Not at my table, of course. Although, I would have liked it very much. At a table beside mine with a piccadilly gentleman of curiously bubbly inclination. He was well-bearded and smiled kind, but his conversation was mere footnote to hers which I must say was of tremendous vocabulary, vivacity, and volume.

She must have noticed that my eyes wandered. Hers did too, and I had the strangest sense of sudden déjà vu. I shook it off, swept at my hair to turn it under my hat and smiled to myself as I waited for the waitress to return with fresh water for my tea and a coffee.

She came from money. It threw me at first. To hear, so proudly, talk of Swiss villas and evenings in Rome. But, I was a bit of a something myself, at the time, so I smirked at the thought of enjoying Switzerland in the winter rather than when it was warm. Progress in the novel fared poorly but it remained good cover, so I fought off every urge to set it down.

I could see the way she smiled. Flashing broad streaks of gleaming white through the corner of my eye, melting into the golden blur of her perfectly wavy hair. I had noticed her in full form, but it seemed I had forgotten what it was that I had seen with each tick of my hand-wound watch. And so, I would check. Half to see if she was still there glancing back, and half to remind myself of the true beauty that I beheld.

In reality, and to be truthful I would later write to my sister, it was not her physical beauty or potential charm that drew my eyes to lust for her over and over. It was this unmistakable confidence. A self-assuredness that I had never seen before, or since, in any other woman or man.

It radiated from her. It drove her. Often, to do more than she ought to have, but. Beautiful. And sometimes. Sometimes, I wonder as I did then in that moment if it wasn't just the sun.

I look back. Turn it over. It is then that I realize. Tears streaming from my eyes like a newborn that it wasn't the sun, but it may as well have. For she was all that it is and was to me, and she was always better with each glance and the longer the duration.

Then and now.

On that day, if I remember correctly, and at times my memory is sparse. Even the most vivid of imagery fails me.

The stream flowed in full force despite the chill. Alive. Quick and silver, a river of fluid flavor and flashing color. Once in a while a bright streak would split and break from the current.

A rainbow like glint splashing forth from the sun drenched surface.

Then back down.

Gone.

An Interview with the American Dream
Chapter 2

"That was how you met her?" Marcus Wells asked as he leafed through a thin album of blackened newspaper articles.

I dug through drawers and tapped my chin, muttering under my breath as I went. They weren't in the filing cabinets. They weren't in the desk. I even dug beneath the pens to the back where I kept my old checkbooks, passbooks, and postcards. Then, I went on digging through them a second time.

He looked up from the pages of faded history and pushed his fingers into his eyelids, "Mr. Kennig?"

"Dan's fine, young man," I reminded him while working on the bookshelf, straightening Russian history novels organized by sub-genre and alphabetically by title. My mind ran through the likely destinations of these sacred relics. It's always when you want something that you can't find it.

"You were saying how you met your wife," he repeated patiently. He was a journalist, as classic as they came, and he wasn't here to read through stiff prose stripped from old articles written for the Times.

"Yes, I was," I hesitated holding a hand to the handkerchief tucked in my shirt pocket.

"You left off at 'thump'. Care to elaborate?" the pen clicked and he bit the tip as he eyed his notes. I turned from the bookshelf and came around the couch to sit opposite the young man.

"I'll certainly never forget her," I said. "She picked up my book and slammed it on the table so hard the coffee spilled onto the saucer." I could feel the blood rush to my skin and run hot like a grade school blush. He chuckled.

"How long ago was that?" he asked.

"Oh my, that must have been nearly 70 years now," I replied. I tried to follow his eyes as he scribbled notes in between prepared questions.

"Don't mind me, but I find it strange that a young woman of those days would do such a thing."

"I think young women have always gone after what they want. I was just lucky that I was what Cynthia wanted."

"An extraordinary woman."

"I'd like to think so," I smiled, "but for other reasons. Young women were good to us veterans after the war."

"So, tell me about that," Marcus leaned forward, "You had just come back from serving in the war. Did you find it hard to adjust?"

"Some. It was hard to find a job."

"Did knowing Cynthia Gold help?"

"I met her later. After I had started singing with my first real night club in New York. Anyway, a friend of the family put me in touch with a modeling agency in the city and I did that for a few months. That's why I moved to New York."

"Sounds exciting." He scribbled something quick-hand.

"Not so much." I hesitated, "I didn't like the people too much."

"Oh, why was that?"

"I felt like a piece of meat. Being shipped around, poked, and prodded."

"Did you do a lot of work for them? I must say I saw some of your photos in old articles. You were a good-looking guy."

"Thank you. I worked mainly for a department store, Childs. Did you ever hear of them?"

Marcus shook his head, "No."

"They were the big thing at the time."

"Never heard of it."

"Funny, isn't it?" I stood up, "Would you like something to drink? I've got gin, scotch, coffee, soda. Even Powerade."

"Water's fine." I could feel his smile through his voice like a gentle wind on a fine day. I went to fix myself some brandy and him a water. Always needed something to calm my nerves when I got to talking about Cynthia. The memories could come on so strong.

He followed me up, "Dan?"

"Yes?"

"I couldn't help but notice you don't have a single photo on any of the walls. Only paintings."

"That's correct." I handed him the water and took a swig from my glass like a sailor.

"Why is that?"

"Well, you see, it was a request that Cynthia had made when I first met her."

"What was that?"

"That I never take a photo of her. Seeing as she's gone, I haven't cared much to keep a photo of myself around either. One mirror is enough for me."

"Why would she ask something like that?"

"She was an of the moment kind of gal. Liked to live life today. Photos reminded her of death. She always wanted to remind herself that she was alive."

"So, she was adventurous. An adrenaline junkie?" He sipped his water, smirking over the rim of the glass.

"Gosh, I hope not. She just had an incredible capacity for loving that you couldn't help but feel inspired by."

"You have no photos?" he asked.

"Not one."

"What do you have to remember her by?"

I laughed.

He had on a goofy grin like he couldn't decide whether he was out of a joke or had to take pity on an old man. I didn't bother putting my finger to my head, but the fit of inspiration had reminded me where I had stored the old things.

I shifted around a pile of trinkets in a chest drawer and fished out a sealed plastic package. It may not have been photographs, but I treasured it even more.

"What's this?" Marcus asked.

"That is a diary, young man."

"I may not have as many notches on my belt as you say, but diaries haven't changed that much."

"It's a--" I sat down. I had to stop. "You'll see."

"What is this from?"

"Cynthia and I." I summoned the courage, "We took an extended vacation together early in our relationship."

"To where?"

A moment in the sun
Chapter 3

Marcus took the letters with him. He probably thought that I was going senile with the way that I had forced them into his hands.

I knew that my eyes could gloss over as if I had gone into epileptic shock. For a long time I didn't move from where he had left me. In my big red arm chair, nursing the brandy. The wind battered against the side of the apartment building, so I got up to close the windows.

How I met her. In a single moment of sure violence, Cynthia Gold took a book from a stranger.

She slammed it down.

Thump.

Her grin widened at the sound.

She spread her arms out over the table. A predator, prepared to pounce.

I sat back. Leaned forward.

"You weren't actually reading that now? Were you?" Her teeth flashed. Her skin glowed. She adjusted, propping herself up proper. The shadow fell from her face. I could see myself reflected in her sunglasses, a black streak in the gold shimmer of light.

"What if I told you that I was, and that it was just about to get real good?"

"I'd call you a liar."

"As a matter of fact I was," I chuckled, putting a hand on the book, "listening to your stories."

"Sounds about right," she shrugged and glanced back at the awkwardly grinning man-boy she had left alone at the other table. "Did you find them interesting?"

"Of course."

"You're one of the boys from the Childs catalogue, aren't you?" her eyebrows curled skeptically over the edge of her aviators. I blushed a full and deep red. "Cynthia Gold." She held out her hand, amused.

"Daniel Kennig."

I extended a handshake and kept it firm. Her eyebrows rose as if a kite lifted momentarily by a gust of wind.

"You don't know who I am, do you, Mr. Daniel?" she crossed her arms. It felt like a blanket of fog had been laid over the table. Under its veil now were only the two of us.

I drummed my fingers on the book, "You say that as if I should."

She mulled over me from behind the impassive glare of golden glass, "No, you shouldn't. It's good you don't. I'll be at the Skylark, the evening after next. Why don't you meet me there?"

"You mean Monday?" I blushed further.

"I like you, Dan," she said.

She stood up to go.

"Monday, then?"

"Yes."

THE SUMMER

Book I of II

Marcus Wells
Chapter 1

I pulled into my garage and opened the car door with the key still in the ignition. I put my phone in my mouth and worked the key out of the slot. The beeping disappeared and then I remembered Daniel's letters. I put the phone in my hand with the keys. Put them both on the chair. Reached over the console to grab the plasticked package and then put it under my arm. Then I remembered my donut. I stuffed the donut in my mouth, picked everything up and then got myself into the kitchenette using my elbows.

It's not every day that you got to hear the life story of a man like Daniel Kennig. His old SoHo apartment was more chic and modern than this 30 something year old moderately successful journalist's Long Island bungalow.

I chuckled to myself. I sat at the worn wooden table wishing that I had cherished my donut longer than a few seconds thinking.

He was still living the sweet life, and yet, the thing that lit up his eyes more than anything was the one thing that he had lived without longer than he had anything else:

Cynthia Gold.

We didn't talk about the awards, the albums, the world tours. Seventy years. I can't even imagine that. My wife and my daughter were gone for the day. With Shawna and Allison gone to work and school, this was my time to be productive.

Be productive. All I needed to do was get to writing this "Last Interview with the American King" and finally solidify myself as a prominent investigative journalist. What would I buy with the first paycheck in a long time? For some reason kitchen tiling came to mind.

I pulled my notebook out of my shoulder bag. There was enough material here to ghost-write two memoirs. Something stopped me.

The Letters.

He had been on the stage for more than half of his life. Six decades of smooth vibrations filled the ears of his crowd with brilliant emotion. Yet, for him, the Man, himself, it all boiled down to a forgotten summer just before his marriage with a fable of upper tier society.

As much as you could find out on Mr. Kennig, Cynthia remained a mystery like Shakespeare's lost years. Granted I hadn't given it much research, but what I had found had been hard to come by still. I knew that the pair had been married. She had a reputation for a will stronger than steel and her taste. She had a known knack for disappearing for months at a time on rather strange jaunts. She was the quintessential Siberian tiger of women.

The complete opposite existed as Daniel Kennig. A booming public persona married to the stage. Throughout his career he made grandiose, sweeping gestures earning him the reputation for being a modern Gatsby in the flesh. How the two of them met and fell in love seemed as unlikely as water on the surface of the sun.

I turned over the package and read the perfect black sharpie aloud, "Letters from my brother." The plastic pulled open easily. I rifled through them quick and then picked the first.

Dear Mary,

There is nothing quite like New York, Mary. Every day there are people who discover the city for the first time, and they come to the same conclusions that we all inevitably have. "I'm here. The stage is set and sitting center. Me. Time to see what I've got."

I hope I've got you laughing now. Sarcasm aside. I know I said I would write sooner, but you see I've been out and around chasing after the daylight like we chased butterflies that one summer at Badger Lake with Josie and Mark.

I haven't had all the time or the words, but know that the weather is right, the city is good, the people surprising, and the prospects bright. And it was just last week on the corner of 11th and Broadway that I met the most extraordinary woman. We didn't talk much then, but we rendezvoused at the Skylark last night. We talked well past midnight. About what, I can't remember. Mostly books, I think. She even invited me to a party here at the Grand.

I do hope that I have quite enough good taste to suit her. I should likely ask Tom for help. Even then, I shan't be disappointed if the company turns. To even be at the Grand for a night will be spectacular.

To be in her presence once more, well, I feel I have gone too far too fast. It will be delightful, if anything. But, of course I wouldn't think to promise anymore. Especially on behalf of one good lady to another.

With Love and Sincerity,
Your Best Little Brother
Daniel Kennig

P.S. It gives me an idea for a song.

P.S.S. I still love you more.

Suave Tom and the Grand
Chapter 2

So, this is how it happened for all of us. Even Daniel Kennig asked a friend with more experience what to do before meeting the girl of his dreams for a third time.

I took a moment to admire the letters. They had been laminated, labelled, and dated. Notes had been scribbled along the sides in another's hand-writing.

It was strange to think. It reminded me of when I first met Shawna. I called Phil's number first. He asked me over to his house where he gave me the run down on the birds and the bees so to speak. I didn't tell my mom about her for months.

So, Daniel had his friend Tom. Suave Tom. They probably met over beers at an outdoor seating restaurant in the sun. I saw it in my head like a speed sketch.

Tom, well dressed and funny, sweeping his hair back. A caricature of a man talking with his hands. He probably wore a colorful tie. Opposite of him stood Daniel. Quiet and serious, brooding over Cynthia like he was going to war.

Tom likely laid down some hard truths and life lessons. Kid, don't back down. When resistance comes, crush it.

One note in particular caught my eye - *Please, anyone but Tom.* At first, I thought of skimming it. Then I read through the whole thing.

"Hmm, that's to be expected," I said to my empty house. Suave Tom wasn't his sister's favorite. Big surprise. She was too far away to give more detailed advice, but avoid Tom read clearly.

Fortunately, her letter warning Daniel away from Tom arrived in New York before he went to the Grand. Maybe he would take her advice. If I remembered correctly from my research, she had stayed in Indiana after getting married to her high school sweetheart. I rifled around for any envelopes to check, and I confirmed that she had.

Dear Mary,

I received your note in time, but it's a waste to tiptoe around it, I kept my date with Tom. Whether you believe it or not, it was a great thing I did. Had I not, I might never have gone. And, you will never believe what happened…

Suave Tom won after all.

* * *

I met Tom to play tennis in the afternoon on Wednesday. It was a good day to take the outdoor courts as the summer heat hadn't set in, and although it had been supposed to rain, the humidity had let up.

The air was cool and the sun was out. It would make for a delightful afternoon.

Tom really took it very seriously. He brought his own gear. Top of the line stuff and opened a new carton of balls for each set. Sometimes, if he thought the volleys were good, he would have a new ball for each game.

It baffled me, but I enjoyed playing and I wasn't so bad. I was bad, but not so bad that a good player like Tom didn't mind beating me. I challenged a set every now and again, but Tom could be really very ruthless charging the net and I couldn't bring myself to run anything down that hard.

He pulled three cartons of balls out of his bag after we had changed and come out onto the court. He counted them off and popped one open.

Tom gave me his guest racket and asked me to pick a side.

"Do you mind playing into the sun first?" I asked.

He shook his head and I noticed that he had that dumb smirk on his face again. It was that kind of I know something about you that you aren't telling me type of look, and he lauded it over the changing room without bringing it out.

"Tom. Are you going to grin like a Cheshire all day or do you have something on your mind?"

"You've ditched the fedora."

"Yes."

"It looked good on you, but this is better."

"Yes," I said. "I agree."

"So?"

"What?" I asked. "Are you going to take your side?"

"Did you meet a nice girl?"

"Hmm," I could feel my face flush, and I felt a little angry.

"Did you mee--."

"I heard you."

"--a gir--. Well?"

"What makes you think I met a nice girl?"

"You've ditched the fedora for starters," he said. I twirled the racket and motioned for the balls. He gave me the open carton.

He let me serve first as a handicap. He had taught me how to full serve, but it had been awhile. If I could land one, I might get an ace. I tapped a ball to the court and back and he smirked again. I frowned at him.

"I guess she didn't have to be a nice girl."

I reddened some more and squeezed the ball a little.

"Out with it then. You're usually chatty."

I bounced the ball again and then put it in my pocket before pouring the other two out and adding one to the opposite pocket.

"I did meet a nice girl as a matter of fact. I guess I'm easier to read than I'd like to be."

"If you don't want to talk about it now," he looked at the other courts where the games were going in full swing. "I've got a game of Bridge Friday evening. You can join us. We can talk in between. Good group. Trustworthy sort. Been meaning to introduce you, but it's a high table and I don't plan to be your sponsor," he shrugged.

"Can't," I said. "Though for once I don't mind the high stakes."

Tom grinned merrily, "came into some money, huh? Did you get an advance from Mickey then?"

I nodded. "Are we going to play? If you don't take your side, I will."

"I want to talk. It's been too long since we got a game in and I feel like I need to know the reason why."

"Old Mickey's the reason why. He's got me singing a show every week, and now his wife wants me to meet with anyone they can market me to."

"That's what happens when you got a face like yours. You don't just meet nice girls anymore." He laughed at his own jab, but I didn't find it very funny.

"Later. Let's talk about it later." I looked over at some of the spectators wandering the club grounds. "We don't have the court all day."

"Fine."

So we played a set. We both got hot and sticky in the sun, but when we paused or stopped running around the clay, the breeze was nice. My serve was strong, but he kept challenging my backhand. We got a few volleys to ten, but I lost each and finally he took the set straight through.

"You're off," Tom said. He came over and tossed me a towel from the bench. I stood at the line waiting, but he gestured me over. "Oh come off your horse and take a seat. What is it?"

"She's invited me to a party Friday evening at the Grand."

He smiled, "good."

"I thought you'd have more advice."

"Leave the fedora at home."

I chuckled, "that's it?"

"Look, Danny boy, you don't need me on this one. You know all the things you need to already. She chose you."

I shook my head, but I didn't know why.

"I'm surprised it took this long, actually. If you want blatant honesty," Tom said.

"What did?"

"You getting hitched, Danny."

"I am not hitched yet."

"Hell, even I've got a ring after a year in this city. And, I was determined," he said. "Determined not to that is. Of all my friends that I would have thought would get married first, it would have been you." He scratched his cheek and wiped his forehead with the towel. "Do you have a plan for when you are at the Grand?"

I shook my head.

"Do you still only have the one suit?"

I nodded.

"Okay good, wear it."

I waited awhile to see if he would start again, but he didn't.

"Now, is that it?" I asked. "Just wear the suit and ditch the hat?"

"Yes," he looked at the court. He took out the new carton of balls and had me fork over the old ones. "Ready to play another set?"

"Thanks." I said.

"What for?"

"Being a good friend."

"Shut up Danny. You never need anyone to talk you out of things. That's not your problem. Not yet anyway. You need people to talk you into things."

For some reason I thought about Mickey. Tom slapped me on the back and took the side opposite the one he took in the first set.

I realized that my palms had gotten sweaty, so I wiped them on my shorts before taking my place on the back line with the new balls.

I started on the serve, and the game went good. Better than the first. I felt loose and the ball sprung off my racket a little faster. He was right. I had been off. I lost the set again, but won a few games.

We went off to lunch afterward and Tom flirted with the waitress since he was only engaged while I took out one of Woolf's classics. We had sandwiches and soup and we didn't talk about Cynthia again. Every time Tom looked at me, he smirked. It didn't bother me anymore though. It made more sense.

* * *

Marcus Wells flipped through to see where he was in the stack of letters. He licked his lips and thought about how innocent the Daniel Kennig of historic fame sounded as a young man. Fated to embark on the journey to fall in love and talked into it by his friend, the cad. He adjusted the pillows on the couch and nestled into the softest corner before delving deeper into history.

* * *

There I was.

The cabs lined up and took off like a swarm of bees.

Light spilled into the street like shaken champagne and splashed across the feet of the dapper crowd that disappeared through the Grand's doors.

I stood off to the side of the entrance listening to the merry laughter of the party goers. Hundreds of the Manhattan gentry descended on the hotel for the evening, and I arrived in the midst of it all.

For a moment, I thought I might be being taken for a ride. She could be playing me. Miss Gold. I, the simple Indiana man, wouldn't know better. I clapped my hands together and noticed their shaking.

I looked into the shiny window to my right, adjusted my tie, ran my hand through my pomade-laden hair and gave myself a nod. I had come to New York for this. To be this. First, the dangers had melted away. Then, the stages and microphones, and clubs. The last step was to find the city's heart and become a part of it.

The red carpet lay out before me and I took the first step after an excited party following a flirtatious little girl with a bottle of champagne. The doors rose up and opened before us. Attendants in white with white gloves bowed and tipped their caps in unison. The faint sound of music and gaiety picked up and beckoned us within.

Their shoes clacked and tapped on the marble floor and then so did mine. Guests leaned against gold balconies to watch the parade. They laughed and pointed. Their forms shimmered and shifted in the sparkling light of the crystal chandelier. I could hear more footsteps on the marble behind me.

Candles lined the oak counters. Damask covered chairs and couches were pushed up along the walls. Someone in the party ahead remarked on the ceiling. I looked up into the twisting light of the chandelier. Little fairies danced along the reds and purples of the dark Renaissance mural.

Stained glass windows refracted moon light into blue on the dimly lit hall before us and the doors came apart gently before we arrived. Another two attendants with gold shoulders on their white uniforms tipped their caps and presented to us, the ballroom, where the music surged into its crescendo.

I took it all in one breath.

The piano. A full grand so richly colored I imagined it was crafted from some rare single-origin wood. Just behind it on the same raised marble platform stood a harp the size of a small elephant made of solid gold.

The dance floor, half full of the exquisitely dressed elite, extended to colored glass that glowed in the light of the chandeliers that hung over each of the large tables cloaked in sheer white satin. Large bouquets of flowers sat dead center lifting the scent of lilac into the air.

Chatting, whispers. Roaring laughter. Sniffs. Smiles. The clinking of glasses and silverware. All so much. All so fast. Everywhere I loo-.

A red butterfly.

My red butterfly, catching my eye after all, sat
with a coat thrown over her shoulders like a cloak
surrounded by a throng of men. Through an opening
I caught her slender profile and her sleeveless red
dress. Her long maroon opera gloves dangled in the
air as she told another one of her stories. Like
Arabian nights, each successive tale became more
fascinating and tangled in the fabric of her life than
the last.

The men laughed. Girlfriends stood at her
shoulders like gargoyles on a gate.

I advanced straight for her. I would not waste
my time idly circling. I had seen all that I could see in
the rest of this place, and if the night was to be any
bit a success I could hope it to be, Cynthia's voice
would make it so. I had a sudden urge to hear it. My
heart pounded. I went to tighten a cuff link and the
glimmer of the silver caught her eye.

She smiled, stopping her story mid-sentence.
She saw me too.

She looked down. Her eyelashes fluttered. She
blushed a little bit when she realized the air had gone
out of the room. Her hands drifted slowly to her
sides. The hungry group of guppies took one last
look at me before turning back to her to see what she
might do.

The calm had settled in me now. I belonged. I
was the one that Cynthia Gold waited for. I motioned
for the waves to part and they stepped aside.

How could I have ever doubted myself? How could I have ever doubted her? Something started had now begun.

"You look cute Miss Gold, but if you want to be King, I might first suggest a crown."

She froze and then relaxed slouching into her chair.

"You're late Mr. Kennig, and might I say you look mighty cute yourself. Much like a schoolboy."

A whistle from our spectators.

She smirked and looked up into my eyes.

I felt like I was melting in place. Like my feet would stick like hot glue and I would slowly sink into the ground watching the world drift away.

The song stopped leaving only the chatter from the dance floor.

"May I have this dance?"

"I quite like that idea. Though I would have danced with anyone who asked me, I'm impressed. I thought you would wait to ask." She put out her hand and I took it. I tried to hold back my smile, but failed.

"Did you take me for one of these guppies?" I asked as she used my weight to help herself stand. She burst into laughter. The coat fell from her shoulders.

She gathered herself with a gleaming glance. We went off to join the dancers as the next song began.

We danced for a song without talking. As soon as the melody took off, we realized that our dancing together would be difficult. Our chemistry until now had come so easily that we each had thought nothing of taking to the dance floor together, but now here with the slow song starting, the flames began to temper.

I could feel her desire to lead through her fingertips. She followed each step but she thought about it too much. Each time I advanced, she hesitated.

I could feel my heart pounding in my chest and hers too through the wrist placed against my side. A faster song began, so I held her a bit more firmly and pulled her closer hoping she would let us fall in together in stride.

It worked. I glanced at her just in time to see a smile drift across her lips.

I led her left and she stepped on my shoe.

"Oops," she said like a little girl whose shoe lace had untied.

I chuckled, "at least you kept dancing little Miss Gold, but next time try not to put all your weight on it."

"You were a little close Mr. Kennig. I needed the space."

"Fair enough," I smiled and pulled her again nearer to me. She didn't resist.

"Be careful, maybe this time I'll bite."

"I guess I don't mind. Your lips would be closer to mine." The words slipped from my mouth before I could even think and I blushed.

"You're blushing," she said with a wolfish smile.

"I know," I said.

"It's cute and unexpected," she said and looked over my shoulder. I blushed deeper.

"With all that confidence over by the table, I thought I'd have to knee you in the gut before the end of the night."

"I'm certainly glad you didn't," I shook my head and then bit my lower lip. She stared into my eyes.

"Nothing is certain. Don't count it out yet."

"Well then I'm glad you haven't, but might I say you should and spare me the heartbreak of having to do it later."

She laughed and held tighter.

I gave her more space. The dancing became easier. I let her lead and she became more compliant.

"Don't fall in love Mr. Kennig. You don't even know me."

"I'm not in love Miss Gold, but what I've seen I like."

"If I requested that we be only friends forever, what would you say?"

"I may forget to write, but it doesn't mean I'll stay away," I said. She looked up, startled. I winked.

"Naughty boy," she slapped my chest. "You've lost your privilege to talk."

She took the lead again and we danced silently through another song.

"Have you had anything to drink yet?" she asked.

I shook my head.

"No?" She tilted her head and looked up at me unbelieving. "You can talk now."

"I went straight to you."

"Did you?" She blushed now and she saw the knowing look in my eye and pulled away. "I'm exhausted for one, so let's get a drink for you and some fresh air for me."

I followed her to the bar where she ordered the drinks. Her comments were abrupt and slightly abrasive, but the waiters ignored it. She got a straight whiskey for herself and two champagne shooters for me.

I stared after her as she weaved between guests placing a firm hand or wrist against their backs, chests, sides, cheeks leading me away from the main doors.

A door came into view beyond the edge of the platform where the band played. It opened with the sound of air escaping from a bottle and a cold gust of wind rushed up my neck and down my back.

I sighed in relief. I hadn't realized how hot it was in there.

Cynthia shook her whiskey and the ice rattled in the glass. She leaned over a balcony and gestured with the glass at the south facing view. I set one of my champagne glasses down and joined her.

"I don't care what anyone says about nature, that's still one of my favorite views."

I mimicked her posture leaning my elbows against the railing and feeling the cold stone through my shirt sleeves.

"I agree," I said.

"We can't just agree all the time," she said and took a drink. "It's not healthy for a relationship."

"I'm glad it's come to that." I touched a nerve.

She winced and said, "I misspoke."

"I didn't mean it that--."

"Oh I know Danny."

I let the air be the only sound in the night. The party slowly quieted as the heavy door behind us fought against the wind until it shut with barely the sound of a fart.

"What is it?" I asked.

"Oh, you're too good, Danny," she said. "Not what I was expecting. Why did I have to go and meet you now?"

"Why? What's on your mind?"

She looked at me and the sudden gravity of her seriousness settled in.

"Are you married?" I asked. She shook her head. "Do you have kids?"

"No, shut up. No," she said.

"Are you seeing some--" I couldn't help myself.

"I said shut up."

"--one. Okay." I sighed and took another drink.

We could hear the band play and the crowd laugh and dance behind us, but it seemed better and more intimate outside under the old gas lamps strung up along the high wall.

We stood there a long time looking together at the lights in the towers blinking on and off. Millions of people living their lives and either realizing or not realizing what they had, but never able to tell which they were at any given time.

"You know I bet you someone out there is falling in love right this second."

She shifted and took a drink. She examined the whiskey as if she expected it to all be gone already. It was half full and the ice still floated around.

"I bet you someone out there is planning to rob a bank."

"Oh, really? I bet you someone out there has a plan to stop them."

"I don't know what to say. I've just met you, but I feel like I've known you my whole life. I wanted to not like you Danny, but now I."

I didn't say anything. She choked back a sob and I looked at her surprised. I brought my hand up to her shoulder, but left it hovering. I pulled it away before she saw, balled my hand in a loose fist, and let it drop to my side.

"It's just I don't want to break your heart Danny."

"What's so hard to say?" I said, angry now, and somewhere between hurt and defensive. She looked up at me. A wave of realization washed over her face and I relaxed.

"I must the leave the city."

"That's all right. When will you be back?"

"My mother wants me to be in London. Permanently."

I swallowed the last of my champagne and it didn't taste so sweet anymore.

"Can't you make the choice?"

She shook her head and said, "Not yet. You don't understand. It's too complicated." It had set in now fully, and I felt somehow cheated by the world of happiness. She groaned and I understood that she did too. "Why London?" she repeated.

"Why? What's wrong with London?"

"Have you been?"

"Yes," I said. I looked down at my empty glass and then set it on the ground. I saw the second glass that I had forgotten and picked that one up. I drank it too real fast and felt like tossing the glass over the side, but I put it down next to the first.

"It could've been anywhere else," she said, "Why not France?"

"What's better about France?"

"I'm assuming you haven't been?" It was good to see her smile again as she took another swig before glancing back out at the city.

"Nope never." A brisk wind hit the balcony. We both shivered, but the city skyline just had that way about it that night and we couldn't look away.

"Everything, I suppose," she took a sip, "But for starters, every one of them I meet can string a full sentence together. Even many in English. How many Englishmen speak French?"

"They have to," I said. "The French I mean have to with the English you know."

"Why's that?"

"Why? They're all such pains in the ass. They have to know English, so they can share their damn opinions on everything." She snorted and I swear she spit out her whiskey.

"I thought you'd never been," she said.

"Not yet, but I've met plenty of Frenchmen." I held my tongue sensing she was waiting for me to list my exploits, but when I didn't she let herself smile freely.

"It feels good to laugh again," she said. "Anyway, there is at least something we can agree on. There are more than enough common people in London who don't take time to read and then complain about not having known."

"Sounds a lot like the States."

"You didn't let me finish," she said and I gestured for her to continue, "I've never met an American who doesn't like to read." I looked at her skeptically, but she lifted her whiskey into the air and gave me a raised eyebrow.

"Have you left New York?" I asked thinking of my hometown in south Indiana.

"Plenty of people visit from everywhere. I've even met people from Oxford," she said, "Mississippi." More certain now than before that she had made her point, she drank her whiskey and nodded with a gulp.

"Maybe they're the ones that read about the city?" I asked.

She looked at her empty glass and then pouted and crossed her arms.

"What? Why are you pouting?" I asked.

"You're just being difficult."

"Of course, but," I stopped myself.

"What?" She looked at me impatiently, "What?"

"You did say that we needed to disagree more." Her face twisted in agony and I felt bad for having not lied to her. "So, what's really wrong with London?" I asked.

"Nothing you're right."

"I never said that. Darling," maybe it was my champagne and her whiskey, but I put my hand on her lower back and she didn't stop me, "What's wrong with London?"

"My mother is there."

"That worries you?"

"Yes, it does."

"Why?" I asked.

She looked at her glass, "Let's get us another drink. Would you like more champagne?"

Her smile was back, but it wasn't the same smile.

"I can come to London," I said. "For the summer." *My damn mouth had gotten me into enough trouble tonight*, I thought, *and on only one glass of champagne or was it two?* The look on her face though was too priceless to trade for even all the diamond mines you could ever find.

Internally, my stomach was in a vengeful knot. All my money and it was a lot and most was already spent, especially on paying rent in advance, came from signing a contract with my manager, Mickey, for twelve shows that I would sing in the city over the summer. I may not have come into the city with the best voice, but Mickey could book me and although this wouldn't be my big break, it was a step in the right direction. First, I had to figure out where I could find the money to pay back Mickey. Then, I could figure out how to cross an ocean for my girl. Not even Tom had that kind of money.

"You can't come to London," she said.

The knot in my stomach loosened, but the pit in my heart grew ten miles wider. I felt like I had recovered from someone reaching in and twisting my stomach only to have my heart magically poof out of my chest.

"But," she was thinking now and pacing. "We could meet somewhere in Europe. I could pull away for a little while, and." She looked at me and stared into my eyes, "Your eyes really are beautiful."

"Thank you. Yours are too."

She punched her sides, "Ahh, why do I have to? Not you, me." She said as if she needed to explain. "We'll have to go separately and meet somewhere. Any ideas?"

"It can't be London?"

"My mother would know. She would find out. I know too many people in London. Too many people know me I should say. I feel like I never know anybody who knows me."

"What about Switzerland?"

"In the summer?" She looked at me like I had said a bad word. "That's a great idea. No one I know would be in Switzerland in the summer."

Part of me felt a sense of curious jealousy like I now had to prove that I could be great to her. What I did should be impressive. At least it was to me, for now. I felt on the back heel, but she was looking at the ground pacing and I recovered my composure by the time she looked back.

"Why don't we meet in Zurich in two weeks?" she said and I nodded immediately like a puppy going after a treat. Two weeks to make up the money for twelve shows. I had some ideas. None of them good ones.

The door opened and a group of four came out onto the balcony.

"Sorry if we interrupted your moment. We wanted to get a look at the view."

And with that, Cynthia slipped back into the party like she had been caught out. I found her scribbling a London address on a napkin. She handed it to me.

"Two weeks. Friday at the airport in Zurich. Write to me what time you'll arrive and I'll be there. If anything bad happens or you can't come, don't bother writing. I'll stay there all day in the airport and I'll know when you don't come and have a fine time alone."

She looked up at me. Her pupils swelled into black moons and her lips quivered. I opened my mouth to speak, but she turned away and ran off like Cinderella at the midnight hour. I looked around. The whole party seemed gone. I checked my watch. It was almost two AM.

I took a seat and put my head in my hands.

Two weeks. Twelve shows. That was, God my head hurt to think with how much blood rushed to it. Between the drinking and the sudden onset of an ulcer. I instinctively drank the closest thing to me. More champagne.

It had to be well over $2000. I'd have to steal 6 cars, take down a few convenience stores outside the city or rob a bank.

I thought of Tom and him thinking I had been hitched. What about that, I thought. I could win a game of high stakes Bridge. It was just a matter of who else would be at the table. With Tom's money, you really couldn't know. *What the hell did I get myself into?*

Old Mickey and the Hearts Club
Chapter 3

I woke in a cold sweat. My shirt clung to my back. I tore it off and threw it against the wall.

I looked up and out the window at the full moon. I was awake now in that hyper state of awareness you get with insomnia. I knew I was tired, but that my body or mind or both wouldn't let me sleep.

I crossed the room grabbed a cartridge case turned cigarette holder, a notepad, and a pencil. I lifted the window and climbed out onto the fire escape and then up to the roof of my Prince Street apartment south of Houston.

I took a seat along a patio the owners had put up to get a better view of the Empire State building. The moon hung to my left. I heard the whistle of a heater and wondered who needed it hotter this deep into April.

I took out a cigarette and lit a match against the brick near my feet. It went out in the wind. I tried the matchbox and cupped my hands around the match until the cigarette lit. I waved it off and flicked the smoldering stub at the empty street not watching it fall.

Sometimes Josh or Red would join me up on the roof, but this time I sat alone.

I heard a police siren from towards the Hudson and an airplane engine overhead then a faint shiver ran up my spine. I stared up at the sky wondering how I hadn't died yet, but then again I was meant for something more.

I took out my notepad and scribbled in some lines I had thought up while dancing with Cynthia and that had just come to me again.

I could bail on the advances and ship out to London for good. It could all be over. I looked at the cigarette as the flame slowly dwindled and ate the paper alive. I knew I would quit someday, but when would be a good time?

It was the perfect excuse to sit outside, to spend time alone or to meet someone new. It gave me something to do. Something to fill the in between moments that weren't meant to seem special. These moments were hard to remember and to plan for and weren't the ones that you captured with a photograph, but they made up the vast majority of life.

When would be a good time for anything? My singing career had this sense of urgency to it like I must get famous young, but it consumed my life. People simultaneously took me seriously and not seriously enough. My big break was right around the corner each day. How could I walk away?

I could let her go.

My red butterfly.

She landed in New York City for but a moment and now the moment's gone.

The sun crested over Long Island.

I flipped the cigarette at the street after the match, then looked at the others in the case and then back down onto the street. I climbed back into my apartment and into bed.

* * *

"You're being ridiculous," Tom said, "I'm not going to let you join my next bridge game to bet your savings on a girl."

"Last time we met you said I'd been hitched," I said, "Now, I need to play in that game and win."

"I'd have to cover you when you lose."

"But I'll win," I said.

"Why? Because fate is on your side?" He looked disappointed when I nodded. "No one wins for sure at a card table except for Wild West cheats, and that ended with guns in their faces."

"What other choice do I have?" I asked.

"You've got twelve shows to pay back? Can't you only pay back four? Does it have to be the whole summer? Why not only go for a few weeks and see how you like it."

"Sure, yes, fine. I guess I could cut down the trip. I still have to get out to Switzerland," I said. "I can only do one or the other not both." I should've conceded that I didn't think of only going for a few weeks rather than the full summer, but I hated when Tom was right. It felt like he was always right about everything.

"She wants you in Zurich by when?"

"Two weeks from yesterday."

He sized me up.

"How'd you sleep?" he asked.

"Horrible," I said.

"I won't cover you," he said.

"I know," I said. Tom, the banker's lawyer, could be a bigger pain in the ass than a French girl who wants a glass of wine at a whiskey bar. He would repeat himself four or five times.

"You'd lose anyway."

"Have to play the game to find out," I said. "You're forgetting I could cheat."

"Shut up. You're the only one I trust to keep your head above the water. Besides, they'd kill you if you did and I won't cover you anyway."

"I thought you said they were trustworthy?"

"I did. They are." He said it and meant it and it half clicked what he meant. I figured it was both best not to ask too many more questions and to let it go.

"Did you want to order some sandwiches?"

"I was thinking of trying this new Chinese restaurant in midtown instead. One of my coworkers is from Hong Kong."

"We're already here," I said. He took out a cigarette. I nodded and took one when he offered.

"Let's go try this new place. It's down Broadway from here. Twelve streets or so, just past Madison Square. We can sit down. I won't cover you."

I put my tongue in between my teeth.

"Let's talk about Mickey. Four shows, right?"

"Four shows," I said and nodded. "Maybe six."

"What's so great about this girl? Every day in this city there are missed chances. A passing glance, nothing said." He looked at me and saw right through all the posturing. I was a goner.

"For once I ought to talk you out of something, but I see that won't happen." Tom said. "Six shows? Switzerland? God damn kid. You sure as hell did always know how to pick the tough ones out in a crowd, didn't you?"

"She picked me."

"Right," he said. "They always do."

* * *

I once heard that when you want something badly enough, the universe conspires to help you have it like an immaculate web of interconnected tendrils of fate. I didn't really believe that though until I had found myself renting a flat in the great New York's Lower East Side.

I had always wanted to be a singer and during the war had sung backup vocals during USO shows in first North Africa and then later in Italy. I had been in the Air Force since a couple years before the war broke out. I had forged my papers and signed up instead of going to college at the naïve and tender age of 17.

When I came back, the only job interview that called me back was for a modeling agency which sent me to New York for the Childs department store.

Just as I was about to quit Childs and New York I ran into a sound director who had worked on one of the USO shows. He recommended me to a jazz club whose owner was looking for a singer and bartender. We put on a good show in that late night dive that most importantly was also fun, and one night in walked Mickey Riley and his wife.

That night I got my first Mickey Riley "you" and I traded the white jackets for a three-piece navy pin-stripe suit in the blink of an eye.

Old Mickey ran the Heart's club in Chelsea and had a reputation for being a manager's manager. In short, he micromanaged. He had an ear for good potential recording talent and famously once sold a singer's contract for the club to an ad agency for their jingle.

It had been just over a year in New York when I met Cynthia and for a while there about the only thing that I had going for me was that Old Mickey liked me. He kept telling me that he could book me about as easy as he could eat his wife's pound cake.

I climbed the staircase to Mickey's office thinking of all the times that he had called me in to chew me out. This time I willingly went to prod the animal.

I knew that greatness was there for the taking. If I sang the right song in front of the right crowd, it would be there, but I still worried that I could be throwing it all away if I went through with it and chased after Cynthia.

"You're shit. Your dive's trash. Your whores are garbage. You can take your damn pride and go to hell." Mickey slammed the telephone down as I knocked on his open door. He waved me in and the young man in the room turned to look at me.

"Walter this is Daniel. Daniel, Walter. I picked up Walter from that place on seventh avenue by Sheridan square. I forget the name. To perform some, what was it?"

"Silent dance."

"Yes, that. Well, Danny boy, it's a little kinky and that's what Manhattan wants. Hell, the world wants it. Sexy is the new classy." He sat there with his thick glasses the size of pocket squares and slowly rocked back and forth. "Oh, you need something."

I nodded.

"Walter, could you a give us a second?"

Walter looked at me and then back to Mickey. He got up and left.

"Mick, we've got to talk."

"This isn't about your song, is it? It's right here." He looked around the desk, "I just need more time. Maybe, two months."

"I've got some business we need to discuss."

"About what kid? Get to it."

"I need to move back the next six performances."

"Whoa, that's a wowzer. Why do you need the six moved? No matter, get me back the advance and I'll take you off the set list. It's a little late in the game, but you're easier to book than eating my wife's pound cake. You know." He patted his stomach with a smile.

"I-." I froze.

"Look, don't come in here and give me that and then just turn green. You're only as good as your word, and you've just told me your word's worth damn near nothing."

"I can't do that." I said. "You see I met a girl."

"Yeah? And is that supposed to change my mind about, the advances?"

"She wants me to go to Europe with her." It was all I could stammer out underneath the pressure of Mickey Riley's stare.

"You what? You got to be kidding me. Of all the crazy things people have said to me in this office in my thirty years. You, of all people getting tripped up on some girl?"

"I'd like to make a deal." I stood there wondering where to put my hands. He stared blankly.

"No deal Danny," he said, then a flicker of life flashed on his features. "You know what, on second thought, let's hear it. What's the deal?"

"I'd like to exchange six shows this summer for six in the winter. I could be persuaded to do more."

"You," he pointed his finger at me. I could see the pressure build as he tensed. He relaxed. "That might not be such a bad idea."

"It's not?"

"It might be good for you in the end. A little heartbreak never wasn't. Granted it might not work."

"What won't?"

"Look Danny. It's no secret. I can book you here all right and sometimes at another club, but you don't really have it yet." He tapped his ear. "You're not quite there, but I've had a project on my mind and I've thought of you for it. A friend of Bethany's who is looking for talent. She, my wife, thinks you'd be good, but."

"But?"

"You don't have it, Danny. Not yet. Maybe never." He leaned back. He sat there for a moment staring. "I like you kid. I think you could do something good. Maybe not great. Definitely not special, but good."

"Well, what's this got to do with moving my shows?"

"You know it doesn't work that way. I don't know why you're asking. Probably someone told you that, but look, if you impress Bethany's client, it'd make me more money."

"Sounds grand."

"It's not all a fairy tale. You'd have to go on the road for eight shows across America during the winter."

"Fine."

"This isn't that type of deal Danny. This isn't the type of deal where you're reluctant to accept. This is the type of deal where you cry out in joy, because I've never made this type of deal before. If I dealt with men of poor character and morals, I'd be out of business, but I know you're a man of God and a real one too. None of that hidden private life bull. Hell, we go to the same church."

"I want the deal Mickey."

"Okay, sheesh. Settle down. Look, I'll tell Bethany and let you know within the week. Can you do the next show? The one next Thursday night?" He kept pointing the finger he had stabbed through the air at me and smiled.

I mulled it over.

"What's the earliest I could meet with Bethany?"

"Let me give her a call now and let you know at rehearsal tomorrow morning. In the case you end up doing the Thursday night show."

"Could we move it to this Thursday?"

"On three days prep? Deal."

* * *

I spent the Friday morning taking the train up and down Manhattan trying to forget all the things on my mind while reading Henry James.

Something Tom had said about chances and then all the things that Mickey had said that really pissed me off. How I could only be good. I really hated when people did that. Told me what I would amount to like they could see the future.

I could be nothing or something. I don't care. Just keep quiet about it, because we don't live in tomorrow. He hadn't even read my song.

Eventually, I got off at West Fourth Street and walked over to Café Figaro north of Houston. I sat there with an espresso and my book thinking about the night. Occasionally, I caught a glimpse of a cockroach watching me from the gutter hoping that I'd toss food at it.

Mickey's wife, Bethany, me, and this mystery woman would be dining later that evening at a nice Italian restaurant in Bowery. Barbarino's. I couldn't shake this horrible feeling in my gut, but my heart raced when I thought of Cynthia.

I had to go.

Besides, if I didn't make it to Switzerland, I could potentially be leaving my true love at an airport alone in a foreign country.

A town car pulled up in front of my building on Prince Street around 7pm.

"Get in," Bethany said as she leaned across the back seat of a town car dressed to the nines with white opera gloves, a pearl necklace, and sparkling diamond earrings. She could've been arm candy for anyone at the Grand the other night. Instead she had saved the dress for meeting with this friend.

I slipped in to the seat beside her and she crossed her legs and looked at me. She had this pursed lips look on her face like she was evaluating a foreign meal that didn't come quite as expected.

"Daniel," I smiled and held out my hand.

"Bethany," she said and shook mine.

"I believe we met once before, Mrs. Riley."

"Driver, take us to Barbarinos." The car lurched and eased back into traffic finding its way in the grid with a certain melodic ease only appreciated as a passenger. She rolled up the dividing window and settled back into her original posture facing me on the seat.

"Do you like these buttons?" she asked and she showed off a pair of buttons on the chest of her jacket. She puffed her chest out and said, "Aren't they cute? I sewed them on myself." She leaned a little closer maneuvering for me to get the best look at her chest.

I couldn't resist a passing glance, and my God did I like those buttons but I knew her game and simply said, "They are nice buttons."

"My God you're serious," she said after a long pause, "Look at you. You're as rigid as a board." She put a hand on my shoulder and nudged closer. "Mickey told me you were a serious cat, but."

I couldn't help looking at her legs. Her exposed knee wrapped over the other and her high heels dangling near my left leg.

"Mickey really likes you, you know, but he's upset about this whole business. I think we can have a long relationship if you take care of certain needs."

She nudged closer and she draped her leg over mine. My breath caught in my throat.

"I like you too tiger," she whispered in my ear. "Is there anything you want?"

I looked her in the eyes and tried to hold her gaze as her pupils swelled, "No, I think I'm fine."

"You may find it hard to remain straight and narrow in this business Danny." She put her hand on my crotch. "Especially when I can tell you're interested."

The car pulled to a stop.

I could feel her warm breath on my ear as she lingered there. Her fingers pressed into my thigh. Of course, I wanted to grab her chest. I turned to look her in the eyes and opened the door.

A cool wind from the night flew in. She cooled. I stepped outside and offered her my hand. I had passed the first test. Barbarino's awaited.

I followed Bethany inside. The staff took our jackets to the coat check and gave us bronze tokens. I gave them a tip and we followed the maître d' to a table for four in the back where a young woman sat with an astute older gentleman who must have been in his forties. Her head excitedly scanned the room while he remained impassive. Had Bethany not been making her way toward them behind the maître d' I might have mistaken them for a father and his daughter.

"Bethany!" the young woman exclaimed.

"Lucille! How are you dear?"

They embraced. The young woman's eyes drifted towards mine and when she saw me her face flushed like a school girl who had been out in the cold.

"I am well. And you? Won't you introduce me?" Lucille asked. Her demure voice hid what emotion lie behind her friendly smile.

"Lucille, this is the young man that I was telling you about. Daniel Kennig," Bethany looked at me, "Meet Lucille Long. Lucille, Daniel."

We shook hands and she curtsied and then introduced the other man as her agent and manager, Gordon Fiorlini.

"Shall we sit?"

The pair had opened a bottle of white wine, so the dinner began with that, bread, butter, and progressed quickly into red wine and oven-cooked steaks.

Lucille and Bethany did most of the talking since they hadn't caught up in a month or so, and in between they smiled at me and brought me into the conversation asking questions about my time working with Childs in the city and growing up in Indiana during the depression.

When dinner had neared its end, Lucille requested milk chocolate pudding and ice cream.

"Oh, I did miss milk chocolate these last few years. How about you Daniel? You were in the war, weren't you," she said. "Was there anything you missed while away from home for the war?" Bethany, horrified, looked from me to Lucille who stared expectantly.

"If you don't mind, I would rather not discuss it," I smiled used to innocent inquiries, "If we could talk about why I'm here, I'd appreciate it."

"Well?" Bethany asked looking at me.

"I was under the impression that there was the potential that we could be working together," I said and put the napkin from my lap onto the table.

Lucille's eyes lit up. "Yes, there is," she said.

"But, if you don't mind, I'd like to hear you sing first before we commit to anything." Gordon said, "Could you come by our studio late next week and sing a few songs?"

"I can't. I intend to be out of the country soon. Would early in the week work?"

"We are doing a show in Boston."

"Well what about now?" Gordon asked. We held our breath. The girl's eyes fell to her glass. He continued, "If the boy can sing, sing now."

Bethany laughed, "He certainly can, but we're in a restaurant." She looked around.

"Come now. I'm only needling. No need to worry. The boy looks too straight to break out in song." He eyed me in kind of an off-hand sort of way.

I stood, finished my wine, and started.

And, when I was done, Lucille had that look in her eyes again when we'd first walked in. The rest of the restaurant had joined in.

"I'm impressed," Gordon said. "You certainly livened the mood in the room even if you needed to be a little tight first. We can work with that."

"I said he'd be good. Didn't I Lucille?" Bethany said.

"You did," the girl said, still smiling to herself.

"So what are you looking for from me?" I asked as I sat down and adjusted my tie.

The girl's eyes stared up at me with youthful glee and I couldn't stop looking at the twinkling like little diamonds hung in the light. My stomach dropped, and all I wanted to do was leave the restaurant.

"Gordon?"

"Eh-hem," he cleared his throat, "We'll be doing a cross-country tour. We have seven shows booked now and want to make it a clean eight."

"Tell him how big are the crowds."

"Yes, of course, you see, Lucille here is on the up and while you're good, you don't have it as well as Lucille. I can hear it in your voice. It's not there yet."

"And the crowds?" I asked.

"Yes, well, they line up for her. We'll play to at least a hundred each night, with a show in Las Vegas on the strip that could be two and a show in LA that could reach a clean grand," he smiled at my expression.

The figures ran through my head. I was speechless. This could be my big break. All the butterflies and worries were gone now.

"What are you thinking?" asked Bethany.

"I'm in." I said.

Gordon had them fill the glasses with more wine, "To new friends."

* * *

That night I posted a letter to the address I had received for Cynthia in London.

The awkwardness of the letter made it difficult to write. I felt embarrassed to put the news down and left out all the parts about Mickey, Bethany, and Lucille. Within my heart, I knew I should spill it all, but when I read and re-read each draft, I cut more and more until all that was left was:

I'll be in Zurich on Thursday.

--Daniel.

London Home
Chapter 4

The only problem Mary is that I was to be in Zurich on Thursday and she said that she would plan to be there the next day. What am I to do if she isn't there? I guess I could sleep on a park bench if I can't find a suitable hotel.
With Love Tenderly,
Danny

I looked up from the letter from Daniel to his sister about going to Switzerland and wondered about Cynthia's side of the story. I lazily lay back against the couch and propped my feet up staring at the ceiling.

We had replaced the old plaster with drywall, so instead of seeing faces and figures in the cracks all I could see was empty beige like an acrylic canvas.

My eyes drifted to my desk.

Four!

The bus!

Allison would be just getting off the bus now.

I threw on a light jacket, grabbed my keys, forgot my phone, almost forgot to lock the door, and took off the cul-de-sac for where the bus let off kicking up autumn leaves as I scampered across the lawn.

I knew I looked like a madman, but I ran my ass off. I had never been late for her before. I knew that there would be other parents there, but how embarrassing? Just after we moved to a new neighborhood too. I would never hear the end of it from Shawna, and even if I could forget the condescending look on the other parent's face, the disappointment in Allison's eyes would be fucking terrible.

I rounded the corner and the bus hadn't come yet. I slowed to a walk, adjusted my collar, and rubbed my neck. That was too close for comfort.

I desperately wanted to crack my knuckles, but one of the other dads smiled at me.

"Just wake up from a nap?" he asked.

"Some light reading for work," I said.

"Oh," he frowned and I didn't know what I had done to upset him. No one else spoke then and I wondered to myself if the rest of them were off work, out of work, or househusbands.

There were a couple ladies there too, but they had resting bitch face worse than an Eastern European hooker so I steered over to a spot away from the fire hydrant.

I didn't have my phone, so I awkwardly looked for a place to put my hands without folding my arms like a wannabe tough guy or sticking them in my pockets like a lazy jackhole.

Thankfully, the bus came around the corner and that wave of relief when you know your kid's safe washed over me like getting buzzed followed by the sudden pang of fear that she might not be there.

The bus pulled to a stop. A few little boys came out and ran to their parents. Allison with her fluffy little brown hair came out talking to this blonde pale girl and gave me a big goofy grin.

I felt tears welling at the corner of my eyes as she yelled "Hi daddy!" and ran up to me. I picked her up and stared into her eyes. We started up the road.

"You'll never guess what happened to me at school today!"

"You lost a tooth?"

"How'd you know?" she giggled and I could see the aura of her warmth fill the air.

I opened wide and pointed at one of my own teeth, "I could see this one was gone when you were smiling." I tickled her stomach and asked, "What happened?"

She told me about the playground and the boys wanting to play a game of soccer with the girls, but the girls controlled the jungle gym and wouldn't come down. One of the boys tried to sneak in through the monkey bars and boom.

"Sounds like it hurt."

"Nope, just fun."

Just fun I thought. If I tried that now, I'd end up with 5 weeks of bed rest.

"What'd you do today, daddy?" she asked.

"I met Daniel Kennig today honey," I said.

"Who's that?"

I reddened. It was always embarrassing when a six year old asked you who a singer was for some reason even though you'd explain to them in a heartbeat who a painter was for example. It always made me feel dated and old.

"Mr. Kennig is that guy who sings all the old songs like Sway and Beyond the Sea. You know, 'I've got the world on a string and I'm sitting on a rainbow.'"

"Does he do that Christmas song mommy likes?"

"Chestnuts roasting on an open fire. Jack Frost nipping at your nose." I gave her an eskimo kiss and realized that we had walked past our garage.

"What was he like?"

"Old."

"Was he nice?"

"Very."

"Does he have a wife?"

"Not anymore."

"Does he have a mommy and daddy?"

I shook my head unable to bring myself to give her a darker full truth.

"He must be lonely."

"I don't think so."

"I think he's lonely."

"Okay," I said, "Do you want something to eat? Drink?" I asked. The door shut behind me.

"Butter noodles," she said.

"Again?"

She nodded and sat up on the counter with her chin against the cold granite staring at me, "I want butter noodles." She slammed her fists down and they made dull but painful sounding little thumps.

We talked while I boiled the water, filled it with noodles, and then later mixed in the butter.

"More!" She yelled at me when I only put in a tablespoon of butter.

"Is this enough?" I asked.

"No! Daddy. More! More. More. More. More!"

"Fine. I get it." I conceded by putting a stick of butter in.

"Yay!"

When the bowl of noodles was finally in front of her, she scarfed it down like a cartoon character. I gave her a second helping when she asked for it and then a third. She was so tiny that I kept underestimating how much the little tyke could eat.

"Done?"

"Yes," she said and ran off to watch TV or read a book in her room.

I settled back at my desk ready to do some reading of my own. The letters. Where was I? That's right. Daniel had just gotten on a plane last minute to Zurich without as much as a forwarding address.

It was a different time in those days. People talked in the aisles on airplanes, laughed with the stewardesses, and showed up at hotels without reservations hoping to negotiate a good rate for a night or a weekend.

How stressful must it have been to get on a plane bound for another world hoping a girl you had just met would be waiting on the other side? Then again, he had flown more bombing runs than just about anybody else in the history of war.

Stress and airplanes seemed to find common ground in Daniel Kennig. Still, would she be there? That was the question.

* * *

The gate opened to my family's estate in London. Hopeful buds colored the great oak trees that framed the cherry façade and rustled in the wind. The limousine bounced on the cobblestone and pulled around the fountain. In the cool weather, clear water still sprayed in gorgeous streaks through the air and into the dark pool below lined with pink marble.

Finally, I had arrived.

It was merely a chance meeting in New York after all and it made no sense to me what I had been feeling, but the family home that I once dreaded was such a welcome sight that I felt myself loosen where I didn't know that I had been tight. My stomach suddenly felt empty and needed to be filled.

"Miss Gold," the driver bowed. I exited making sure to press my heels down on the flat stone rather than the sand between. My shoulders felt increasingly warm and tender like they had been held taut.

"Take my things in, will you George?"

"Yes, mam."

"Is mother in?" I asked as a courtesy.

"Afraid not, mam. She's taking the evening in at the Royal Albert. She asked that I fetch you here and let you know that she had a booth with Sir Lucas."

"Didn't have the decency to meet me on arrival, but then expects to snap her fingers and have me anywhere in the city on a moment's notice?" I breathed feeling the muscles snap again back into rigid harmony.

"What was that, miss?"

"Nothing George. Just set my things inside."

"Do you intend to go out tonight?" he asked wondering still if he had to keep the car warm or could retire for the evening. Sir Lucas always dropped the lady Winifred off at home.

"No."

"If your mother asks?"

"Regrettably, George, I am much too tired for entertaining tonight."

"Are you sure? We could have some tea for you."

"I'm not in the mood for yet another opera at this hour after just having flown eight hours in a sterile capsule listening to idle chatter."

"Should I tell her you were sore from the flight?"

"Wonderful idea," I yawned and left much unspoken.

Tell her what you must, I thought, she'll throw her fits whether it's the truth or not. That was her way, and it was just like George to shirk off any responsibility beyond coming up with an excuse on his own. Even if I had more energy, I would not have wanted to waste it listening to more idle chatter in a box seat.

"Good evening Miss Gold."

"Fine to see you Mr. Kent. It has been too long," I went to embrace him and he broke his calm regard for the moment before George entered. The stodgy old butler liked to play the role of the silent sentinel, but he always broke in private.

"Indeed it has. Welcome home. If you don't mind George, I will take Miss Gold's things from here."

"All right sir. Have a good evening Miss Gold."

"Good evening George." I said. He walked off to take the car in and I turned to Mr. Kent. "Is Mrs. Tabernathy here? I could certainly use a bath too."

"She is in the kitchen baking you a surprise. I will have your things sorted and sent to be cleaned."

We parted as old friends do even though he had been the third parent in my life between my traveling father and high society mum. It had been midway through pre-University schooling that he had begun to treat me as an adult and a simple friendship had blossomed just like the one I shared with the head cook, Mrs. Tabernathy, whose eldest daughter had been like a governess to me when I was younger.

Mrs. Tabernathy was a strange thin woman, with arthritic hands, that made the most awfully decadent sweets. Each bite seemed to take me closer to heaven in flavor and health, but somehow her fingers remained as bony as ever.

"Miss Gold! How good it is to see you finally," she said, "I am making you cinnamon buns with spiced pecans."

"You are too good. Did you know that?"

"Oh hush child and go upstairs. We had them put a bath together for you." She saw my surprise and said, "George insisted that he know whether you would have liked to go to the Royal Albert for a new show that they are putting on, but Mr. Kent and I knew."

She gave me a spoon full of hot caramel-like sugar and egg just mixing with flour. The batter melted on my tongue.

What had kept me away so long?

* * *

I came down the stairs in the foyer as the eastern sun cracked through the arched windows spreading little diamonds across the mahogany lacquer that danced in front of each footfall.

I heard the clinking of glass and silverware in the drawing room and drew up against the banister.

Shoot.

Mother had an early guest. Dressed but without having completed my hair. I found a reflective surface to straighten my summer clothes and pull my hair into a bun.

I drew my chest up and arched my back, taking a deep breath and then holding it. The formidable frown gradually straightened into a practiced smile. I knew that it was as false as grandfather's teeth, but if I could convince myself for a moment, maybe I could get through breakfast. I heard footsteps along the tile and spun on the sound.

"Mr. Kent!" I whispered and ran over to the hallway. Alarmed, he turned and ushered me away from the drawing room door.

"Who is that in there?" I asked. My voice whistled angrily through the still air.

"Fitzwilliam, Sir Lucas's son. You must have met him before," he said looking over my shoulder at the cracked doorway.

"What does she expect me to do? I've just been on a flight from New York?"

"Entertain darling. Always entertain," he said and then unconvincingly added, "You look grand dear. As always." I checked the hallway mirror and threw my hands up in the air. I was a mess.

"Is Mrs. Tabernathy--."

"In the kitchen, yes, but don't keep your mother waiting. She sent Elizabeth just now to fetch you." I stood there contemplating, looking again at the stark face in the mirror. The sharp, half-starved lines of my high cheek bones cut decisively through the darkness like the silhouette of a dancer in a black and white flick.

"I suppose," I said.

"I'll leave you to it," he said and went off toward the study annex for whatever purpose I couldn't say. It had dawned on me in that moment why I had loved New York so much and came home so little.

I was completely and utterly alone here. They couldn't even wait a day to remind me. My closest family was hired help and my mother had already brought the latest suitor to the door step to pine for my hand.

Sir Lucas's son? It was no use in pretending that I didn't know what she was about. My father, bless his innocent and loving heart, a good Midwestern boy from Michigan had set in to place two trusts: one that provided a stipend for my mother and another larger one for me.

Of course my mother had used my income as well as her own, and therein laid her problem. When I turned 20, I became the sole authority of the trust. My money became mine alone and she would lose more than half of her income.

However, if I got married before I turned 20 to someone of equal or greater status as my father at his peak, she would inherit the whole will or at least require a dowry of near equivalent value from the groom's parents.

It was not all bad. Only it had resulted in this constant parade of fools. None of them was as sophisticated as he led one to believe. None of them was as smart as his Oxford degree was supposed to make him.

Where did Daniel lay on the spectrum of rich and poor, I wondered.

"Cynthia," Elizabeth whispered, "are you all right? I saw you standing there and thought." She paused, "Your mother sent me to fetch you. Would you like to follow me in with the tea?" She pointed at the fresh set.

"Yes, of course Elizabeth." I forced on my best smile and stepped aside, "after you."

"The lady Cynthia," Elizabeth smiled wanly as we entered the room. Fitzwilliam was dipping a biscuit into his tea. He looked up and stood instantly. He smiled goofily and set down his saucer. He checked the white gloves of his uniform for stains and then looked again at me with the same grin.

"Miss Gold. It is my pleasure," he bowed.

"The pleasure is ours," I curtsied, "mother would you please be so kind as to introduce us?"

"Why this is Sir Lucas's son, Fitzwilliam. You must have met him at the ball last summer?"

"We didn't meet, Mrs. Gold. I would have remembered certainly," Fitzwilliam said.

"Sure you did," she said and pursed her lips. She took up her tea, "Would you two have a seat?"

"Yes mam," Fitzwilliam said. I took the chair across from him as he leaned off the couch to spread some jam and butter on a slice of bread. His hands shook. He put the bread down and ate the tea-softened biscuit.

"Winifred is fine dear." Mother reminded him but only after he had cozied up to her.

"Of course."

"Fitzwilliam and I saw an excellent Opera last night, didn't we?" She looked approvingly over the kettle as Elizabeth poured into each cup.

"Yes, it was goo-."

"His father was indisposed you see. Oh I'm sorry, Fitzwilliam. Were you going to say something?"

"No, it's fine."

"We wanted you to join us. It would have been great for you to spend some time together. Why don't you tell Cynthia what you were telling me about the play? Cynthia spent a decade studying opera in school. She's been attending lectures at Columbia for Art History."

She started dipping her biscuit and sipping her tea without looking up. I had half the nerve to walk around the table and slap her. She made the whole affair sound like some whimsical fantasy of a lost youth. To her receiving a Columbia degree at the age of 19 meant nothing.

"Oh, all right," he said as if prodded. "It was such a romantic spectacle you see," he began and I instantly drifted away in the monotone of his voice. He had a pretty face, almost too womanly. Vibrant, young eyes. They reminded me just slightly of father's although they were a little droopy and cocksure in their innocence.

"You're talking about the Comedy of the Republic?" I said.

"Yes," he said.

"Isn't that the parody of Rome's collapse juxtaposed on parliament?"

"Yes, but you see with the way they create obstacles for the young official who has the affair with the Prime Minister's wife, you get this sense of the grand theatrical narrative inherit to romances at the early turn of the century. It's a little dated of a piece or style, but it has its merits," he explained.

"He is really quite astute, isn't he?" Mother said.

"Yes, please tell me more," I lied.

"I must admit I have seen quite a few productions over the years," he professed, "but I am really no great critic like Scarborough."

"Yes, Scarborough," I said and I caught a glance from mother. I couldn't help it. It was as if all my years of study meant nothing, and he saw fit to teach me about my own field. As he continued, I found myself comparing him to Daniel after his each breath and gesture. I listened and asked questions but my mind drifted.

He had a certain way of telling me how everything was, but not how everything happened. It was as if we were always starting the story at the next point rather than diving deeper into it. The more he said, the more I wondered whether he had really seen the play at all.

"Sounds very sentimental," I said and yawned. He took it as a compliment. "Mother, I'd like to take a walk. Would either of you care to accompany me?"

She shook her head. "Fitzwilliam?" she said.

"I'd love to go for a walk."

* * *

I waved from the front step. Fitzwilliam drove off smiling like a schoolboy who had his first kiss. He didn't look back until he had passed through the gate and out of view.

"You could have been nicer," mother said as the door closed behind me. She watched the expression on my face with distaste, "We aren't commoners. No one marries for love anymore. Not in this world."

Didn't you, I thought, but didn't say. My mother and my father. What an imperfect pair, but what a stranger story they had made. Mom had grown up middle-class in London and brought him out here to play gentry as if the world was always stuck in a Jane Austen novel.

"Well?" She looked at me with a disappointed glare. "Do you have something to say for yourself?"

I didn't. Her words had a distasteful bite that I didn't quite understand. What did she expect from me? Wasn't I the one in the right here? I couldn't understand. My voice caught in the back of my throat.

"I should've known as much. I'll have to make my apologies to Sir Lucas on your behalf. You could at least try to act the part of a woman. You could never take any responsibility for yourself just like your father."

She marched off leaving me breathless. Half of me wanted to be angry and the other half wanted to forget everything that she had just said. I was successful enough, but I could never stand up to her. Her self-righteousness intimidated me.

The foyer emptied of sound. I stood there alone with my heartbeat as the afternoon sun left the enormous room, now dark and lonely. The air hung stiff. Defeat filtered in like fog, but didn't close its icy grip fully. I had been left wounded in battle and forgotten.

* * *

"I can't help but think she must be right, Devlin," I confided. "It must be me. I am doing something wrong." She only wants what is best for me after all. The thought ran through my head, but I held my tongue.

"Oh, shut it, Cynthia. You always get like this whenever you're just home," Devlin said.

"She keeps trying to marry me off. I didn't have a day to rest this time."

He kept silent simply rubbing his bangers in steaming black beans, "You are always so hard on yourself, Cynthia. Forget it and eat your breakfast."

"Brunch," I said. "That's what they call it in the States."

"Well, you do enjoy it there," he replied and cut up a hot banger before putting it on a slice of toast.

"How's Darcy?"

"She's fine. I mean. I didn't really know how to put this or when to say it, but there's never really a good time. She may be pregnant."

"Oh, but Devlin that's wonderful news."

He shrugged, "I'm not so sure. She's a bit young."

"Wait, have she and Darren been married yet?"

"No, but we're certain they will now and soon. It came as bit of a surprise to all of us."

We talked through it awhile, and the news seemed to get better as we dug deeper into the story, "And what about you? Are you seeing any one?"

He blushed, "Yes, a girl by the name of Kendra who goes to school with me in Cambridge. It started a bit slow, but she writes me near every day now."

"I wish I had someone that devoted. My mother would have me marry the first man with a pension."

"Your mother just wants you to be happy."

"I was just thinking the same thing."

"Were you? Because it sounded like you wanted to blame her for all the times in your life that you felt alone."

"What do you mean?"

He took a less than tender bite of his sausage and shrugged, "the story's gotten old with you Cynth. If anything could be so good as to be good enough for you, it would be a bloody fine thing. As it stands, it is always that you're looking for Mr. Perfect out there, but you'll never find him. There is no such thing."

"Maybe, you're right," I said. "But." I thought of Daniel and then my hesitancy to talk of love yet unrealized like keeping paper from a flame held my tongue.

"But?" he stopped eating. The abruptness made my stomach drop unexpectedly. I looked at my eggs béchamel and put down the fork to take a drink of grapefruit juice. He looked at me impatiently.

"I met someone I like."

"Well, tell me about him." Now, his eyes were on fire like this is what we were friends for, so that he could hear about the one man in my life I deemed acceptable.

"I met him in New York in my last week there at a café just south of Union Square. He had on this stupid little fedora and was reading a novel. Something by Hemingway I think."

"Beautiful and smart?"

"Yes, very," I sighed.

"Did you tell him to write?"

"I told him to come."

"You didn't."

"I did." I sighed again, quieter this time.

"No. Cynth. What are we going to do?" His eyes lit up, "Is he coming here?"

"I told him Zurich."

"What are you going to tell your mother?"

"I don't know."

"You can't tell her the truth."

"I know that."

"Are you going to Switzerland?"

"Yes of course."

"When?"

"Three days. I said Friday. I want to be there early in case you know something happens. I've already bought the train tickets."

"Your mother will find out."

"Devlin," I said and he knew then what a portion of this meeting was all about. "Devlin." How were we going to get me to Switzerland without mother finding out?

"He isn't rich?"

"I don't think so."

"So, he's not Mr. Perfect?"

"I didn't ask him."

"Do you think he was in the war? He is an American after all."

"He must've gone to University."

"Your mother," he stopped himself. We had private common knowledge of the situation. The two of us. Mother wouldn't admit it, but we knew that even Devlin's family was considered too 'inadequate' and we shared the same youth college. "Do you remember Julie? She had two younger sisters who liked to sit together in that copse outside the campus."

"Yes. I remember her."

"She just wrote to me that she is off to Marseille with them and wouldn't mind company. You could write a letter and explain to her the situation."

"My mother reads my letters, but I could send two. One from the post office," I tapped my chin. "Oh Devlin, you devious man. You've come up with the perfect plan."

* * *

"I heard that you were going to France," Fitzwilliam said. He looked at me with a hopeful, half-hurt look like he expected something more from me. Some kind of participation in a farcical fantasy that I knew I couldn't give and he wanted to be cordial but it came off as moderately disingenuous.

"I am yes."

"Where to?" He asked, shaping his pleasant face into an awkward half-hearted attempt at a smile. He paced behind the couch as I sat on the drawing room chair leaning an arm against the polished wood and idly tracing the floral pattern on the cushion with one of my fingers.

"Marseille."

"For how long?" he said and added, "I would like very much to see you again when you return," when I didn't answer immediately.

"Oh, not long at all," I said. "Would you like to go for a walk? I think that I could use some air." I said it mostly for his sake, but as we walked out into the small garden behind my family's estate, the cool spring air swept tenderly against my chest and ankles.

"I had hoped to see you again sooner," he said. He looked calmer now and the tempo of his voice smoothed out. I stared at his eyes while he put his hands in his pockets and looked around at the rows of trees.

"You never called," I said.

"I sent along an invitation to the May ball."

"I'll be in Marseille."

"I know that now. I had to ask around."

"Fitzwilliam, you fool. Don't you know you should always ask a girl in person first?" I could see the realization set in and I too grasped finally that this was his first time playing the role of suitor. At that moment my wary regard for the general eagerness at which he plunged into conversation evolved into a mother-like pity.

What had mother been thinking? Did she know? She had paraded all sorts of men at me, but to have challenged this young man with me first? I sighed.

"What is it?" he asked.

"Oh nothing," I lied and walked over to one of the benches. In the summer with all the leaves out it would be hidden from the house, but through the nearly empty branches I could still make out the second floor windows. "Why don't you sit down," I patted the spot beside me.

"My apologies for not having asked you in person," he said at last. I looked at him. Objectively, he was handsome and if he was Sir Lucas's son he was probably in line for the throne. He could be as low as 60th, I estimated.

It was endearing that he hadn't touched or alluded to it yet. It showed good character. Sure I guess I could marry him if I had to. He was handsome and rich, but I wasn't even 20 yet. There was so much more life to live.

"It's quite all right," I assured him and for a little while we talked about the trees.

"When do you leave?"

"Tonight."

He looked back to the canopies and rested his rigid back against the bench.

"Could you do me a favor? Whenever you are back in town, could I accompany you to the Summer Ball at the beginning of June?"

"Yes," I said impressed by his persistence, but suddenly filled with guilt. I checked my wristwatch. "I'm sorry Fitzwilliam, but it is getting late. I really must finish preparing to make my train."

"Could I see you off at the station?"

"No," I said having recovered my senses. I knew I didn't owe anything to Daniel, but what would he think if he knew that I was entertaining other suitors with such serious intentions? There was no guarantee that he would show up in Zurich on Friday, but if he did, there was no mistaking that he had the serious intention to commit to me. For the first time in my life that filled me with warmth.

"Let's walk inside," I said wondering if I had missed something that Fitzwilliam had been saying.

* * *

Marcus put down the letter Cynthia had written her friend about Marseille and thought about how fragile fate seemed to be. It had just sunk in how many obstacles stood before the young pair. Class, country, careers. With each came so many prejudices and principles.

And yet, when Daniel had spoken about her, he didn't talk about hardships or challenges, he had looked like Allison showing me her favorite cartoon characters.

* * *

Marcus didn't hear Shawna enter the house. Work had drained her completely and she still had to talk to Marcus about the lack of help he had been with house and car payments. She wasn't sure that she could keep it together on her own. The job's hours were too demanding. She just found out today that she was getting paid less than a colleague whose work she had to pick up because they thought he was a top performer. Not to mention the commute and despite Marcus's moderate success in the past as a freelancer, she needed to know this most recent gig would pay big and soon.

When she got into the kitchen, her heart sunk further. There were dishes everywhere. He needed to start pulling his weight. She passed the laundry room and found that nothing had been done since this morning. It was the one thing that she really needed him to do.

She picked up toys and junk from the hallway as she made her way to Marcus's study.

"Mommy!" Allison ran up and hugged her leg.

"Give mommy a second, Allison, I just need to talk to daddy for a second."

"No, shh," Allison said, "Daddy's working."

"It'll just be a second."

"No, mommy, daddy's doing something important. Shh," Allison said and pulled Shawna into the living room to watch television.

"Okay, honey, if you say so, I will talk to daddy later tonight."

"Yay!"

"Will you help me clean up then?"

"Clean up, clean up, everybody everywhere," she started to sing and for a moment, Shawna's heart melted and the ice that had grown over it fell away. They cleaned the living room together, put the laundry on, and then started on the dishes while Marcus fell deeper into the world of Daniel Kennig and Cynthia Gold.

Sailboats and the train
Chapter 5

I had this sense when I landed in Zurich that we were building up to something and that we were close, but in the grand scheme of things there was always such a long way to go. The feeling had become so deeply entrenched in my chest that speaking became like trying to wrench a ghost from a cave with nothing but a fishnet.

So, as the plane rattled through the air with the familiar chopping buzz of the propellers, I did not partake in the conversations that grew into pods throughout the interior of the bird. Laughter and jokes seemed suddenly trivial. I could only look out at the wintery white plain and wonder again as I always had when riding high in the morning light, what would it be like to let yourself dance among the clouds?

What would it feel like to let the powdery puffs envelope you if only you could enjoy it before plunging down, spiraling toward the ground?

Clack, clack, clack.

The sound of flack echoed in my ears. I closed my eyes only to put to rest what I could not forget. I wished Josh or Red were still here.

When I woke up, the little mountain town on the long lake appeared as we crested the valley and turned in a wide arc to the airport. The hills were turning green and the lake was full of color. Sails in red, yellow, and blue shared the water together like nothing had ever come between them. I saw the grey sky in the distance and stretched to see the mountains that lay in waiting.

Zurich. We meet again.

* * *

The sun glanced off the street. The air was a little warmer than the night before, but it was not too hot. I hung my jacket over my arm and walked leisurely along the street watching all the storefronts come to life. A red and gold cable car rang passed.

Men in white with smiles and rolled up sleeves laid out boxes and boxes of fruits and vegetables. Oranges, apples, tangerines, cucumbers and more ripened in the sun. Waitresses set tables dressed in red or white with candles from open-walled cafés. Barbers, with funny colored mustaches, twisted blue and red striped awnings into place outside their shops to give shade to benches set beside flower pots. The smell of roses wafted through the air like a blessing.

Friday morning. I expected her to be out at the airport early, so I planned the same.

"Good morning, may I help you sir?" The shopkeeper asked in Swiss-German.

"Do you have any yellow roses?" I asked in English.

"Oh, American? Let me play. You know George Gershwin?" He danced when I nodded and ran over to a record player behind the counter. "Do you like Rhapsody in Blue? Okay, we play!" He put it on and we joked as he cut the stems and shaved the thorns off a dozen yellow roses.

"Parfait," I said.

"Merci vilmal," he replied.

I took the bouquet and stopped by Teuscher. Thousands of fake flowers lining the walls of the store paled in comparison to the lively yellow and green of the flowers bending and straightening that I held out from my body.

The shopkeepers smiled warmly and a bright young woman with her black hair tied in intricate ponytails asked if I'd like to try the champagne truffles.

"I know them well. Oh okay, if you insist." We laughed together as we ate. "Could I get two dozen?

Yes, one of those boxes. No the larger one. Thank you."

She wrapped milk chocolate champagne truffles in a green box with orange wrapping and I disappeared again into the lively marketplace.

The light morning wind from the lake drifted up the street and I could feel the world opening up for me. I had been to the East and to the West and now I had returned to the land of the living triumphant and with so much promise.

I caught the trolley to the airport connection.

* * *

She isn't here. I decided.

Smiling faces arrived and left dressed in exuberant and hopeful summer clothing despite a chill in the air. I ran up and down the gates looking again.

There was no Cynthia Gold.

I collapsed in a chair near one of the double doorways with a sigh. I put the flowers, now bent and broken, on the end table beside me and picked up a magazine that lay there. I looked at the chocolates still wrapped.

It was early. Not even ten.

I would sit and wait here.

I should have brought a book.

I cast the German magazine aside, leaned against the chair, and put my feet up on the coffee table in front of me.

I had all the time in the world after all.

The healthy stream of travelers ushered in and out by the ticket masters had little in common, but I found myself counting shirt colors. Then, I switched to looking for women with hats.

Eleven came and went.

I checked my watch and wondered more times than I could count if I had the right Friday.

I looked to see that I had my watch wound. I left my chair for a moment leaving the expensive chocolates and flowers behind to check the time against the wall clock over the walkway to the flights where hundreds of eager faces filed through without so much as a curious glance in my direction.

Noon passed.

At three I opened the chocolates.

They had melted, but only slightly. I hadn't eaten, but I resisted the urge and retied the bow.

At five an elderly group, thankfully, took the seats around me. I played with the flowers and acted like I wasn't listening, but I was glad for the distraction.

They talked of far off countries like they were old friends. America was closer than a cousin, Siam had sent them gifts for their birthday, and Tuva wasn't a brass instrument.

At six they left for their flight leaving me once again alone.

At seven, the sun began to set over the green mountains. I looked out the window as beams of light caught dust in the airport terminal.

Then it was dark. My stomach roared at me, but I ignored it. There was no telling when she would come.

At nine, I gave in.

I picked up the box of chocolates and wilted flowers and walked toward the exit.

There standing in the doorway, rubbing her gloved hands together in a nervous fit.

"Cynthia."

"Daniel."

Her smile came on quick and I felt a surge of relief flow over me like watching fog roll over the fields in the morning. The ice melted.

I handed her the flowers and chocolates.

"Oh my," she said, "They've melted. It's all right." She put her hand on my shoulder recognizing the temporary horror in my eyes.

"They're quite good," I said. My stomach growled.

"My goodness. How long have you been waiting?"

"Not long at all."

"Daniel Kennig, be honest with me. Would you like one?" She ate one of the chocolates and then presented the box to me. I declined, but she insisted until I succumbed and ate one of the chocolates. Then a second and finally a third.

"It's been so long since I had good milk chocolates." She purred as she ate and we walked out toward the train. She hailed a cab.

"How was London?" I searched for something to start the conversation, but she brushed off the difficulty.

"Dinner?" she asked.

"Yes, please."

"Do you have a place in mind?"

"Have you been to Zurich before?"

"Not for years," she looked out the window and for a moment it felt like the air had gone out of the cab.

"I know a place then."

"Where to?" she asked as I told the cab driver, "Bahnofstrasse, s'il vous plait. Vous connais Al Leone?"

"Ja."

The streets passed and we chatted about European food. She was surprised at all the things that I knew about, but I was equally impressed and intimidated by how she seemed to know every place that I mentioned. I felt no longer like a world traveler, but like a visitor, something between imposter and intruder, who participated as an actor or a voyeur, distant in all but location to the developing scene.

We took a table on the street under the lamp light. A pair of cable cars passed as we talked for a long time before ordering. I asked for a café au lait. She requested a long espresso with milk and a French eclair. We watched the shops turn in for the night. One by one the faces of strangers drifted on and soon our food had come.

Coffee became wine.

"Do you want to know a secret?" she asked.

"What kind of secret?"

"It's not dark. I'd like to teach you something."

"Sure," I said, wondering what she might tell me.

"You know how when you eat the prosciutto it leaves a taste in your mouth that goes well with your Merlot but not with my Riesling?"

"Sure," I guessed. It didn't really matter to me, but this was her expertise and it would serve me well to have it for myself.

"Well, if you'd like to try my Riesling, you can take a slab of butter rub it all over your bread like this and voila. Your merlot was delicious," she said after she set down the empty glass.

"You stole it right out from underneath me."

"Oh darling, I thought we could just share everything."

I swallowed the prosciutto that I had been chewing and did the same quickly with her Riesling.

"Where are your bags?" she asked.

"I got here last night," I said.

"Are you staying nearby?" She adjusted her hat and looked longingly toward the lake.

"At the Maison Zuriche down by the lake. You?"

"The same," she blushed and flattened her dress. "I'm surprised we didn't run into each other by mistake."

"It wouldn't have been a mistake. There are no mistakes," I told her.

"That's a healthy perspective." She adjusted the napkin on her lap and then said, "but there are too many things in this world that needn't be."

"Like what?"

"The war." She shrugged.

"Now, I'm not advocating for it, but, well, what would you have in its place?"

"I think love is all there is or should be. Don't you?"

"Well, I guess I believe that's true."

"You guess?" She smiled at her devilish challenge.

"I don't think evil lurks in the shadows. It stands out in the sunshine with nothing to hide, waving its banner high, and sounding each time as it always does, like the best thing to abate fear. It is not love or goodness that quiets the voices of hate, but the swords of the free and mighty. It might be nice to believe otherwise, but the good always need swords."

"That's a good enough answer I suppose," she finished her wine, "but that doesn't mean I agree. Besides, then what truly is evil?"

"I'd certainly like to know. If you meet the devil ask him for me."

She chuckled and then we settled into an easy silence enjoying the night until she stood and said, "Take my arm. We are going for a walk." We paid and left down the street toward the lake and our hotel.

We walked with only the sound of our footsteps. Strength swelled in my heart when she pressed herself against me and rested her head against my shoulder.

Soon, we made it to the park along the shoreline and looked out at the sailboats silently bobbing in the night. Their colorful sails had been wrapped up and hidden beneath blue or grey tarps.

We went along the lake walk arm in arm in the quiet night. Except for the houses along the shore that lit up the far darkness, it was like any other lake in the world. We could see the whole thing under the waxing moon which cast a shimmering silver beam across the middle.

"Isn't now wonderful?" she said.

"Yes."

"I mean the times. Isn't it an interesting time to be alive?"

"Isn't it always?"

"Yes, but now is especially interesting."

"Why is that?"

"I feel like everyone is rediscovering that everything that was good before the war is still what's good."

"Yes, that's true," I said thinking of all the nations represented by our meal together.

"What do you hope for?" she asked. "Now that the war is over and all."

"Something good to happen," I said.

"That's funny," she said. "I never want anything too good to happen."

"Why? That's such a silly thought," I said.

"I mean it would change things."

"Sure, but isn't change good?"

"Not always. I like a place to be the same sometimes and often it's the good things that go."

"What if something bad happens?"

"I've been thinking about that too. That's not so bad."

"No?"

"If things go badly, there is always a chance that they may go good again. It gives you hope."

"I like the way things are," I thought out loud.

"I do too." She pressed herself against me again and sighed, "but things change."

"They do," I said and felt somehow fearful of that so I added, "but I guess that is what makes now wonderful, isn't it?" I could feel her nod against my shoulder and I saw the hotel come into view at the end of a long line of lamps lighting the walk way through the park.

"I don't want to stay in Zurich after tomorrow. I feel like we've seen it all already especially since we've both been here before," she said. "Where would you like to go next?"

"Have you been to Lucerne? It's beautiful this time of year."

"Yes it is, but I've been there so many times," she yawned, "Have you heard of Interlaken?"

I shook my head.

"Why don't we try that?"

When we got to the hotel, we parted at her insistence but agreed to meet for the morning train to Interlaken by way of Bern. She turned away quickly avoiding the awkwardness of waiting for a kiss, and so we spent the night apart but for the walls of the Maison Zuriche.

* * *

At the station in the morning I ruminated on the last decade while Cynthia picked out our tickets and organized our journey. Although the night before the kindling had taken a moment to light, giddy hopefulness for a shared potential filled her voice and in turn it infected me.

We were now a pair together and it came on me, an interminable bachelor, like a wave of relief. Gone were the concerns with chasing figures under pale lights in after-hours clubs on the streets of New York.

To have gone through a hard thing like the war and come back to another thing altogether was unlike anything else that I could explain. The life of a civilian no longer felt difficult. It became instead an exercise in forging purpose and that made it inevitably like the war still ruled our minds unless we were to throw it from us in a fit of furious love.

Here now was that love finally and it became to me like riding fast down a hill in a soap box racer or carried along on a stream. Actions taken at the beginning had chosen which of the paths would be traveled and now I was but a passenger in fulfilling destiny.

"Here you are," she said and handed me one of the stubs. I put it in my chest pocket and put my hand in the small of her back to guide her to the platform.

A crash. We were up the stairs and taking our place in a line for the second class when cries broke out from across the platform. Someone banged on the train door. Threats of violence filled the air. Scurrying feet.

Instinctively, I rushed Cynthia behind a cement pillar to our right and set her down on a bench.

The train on the other end of the platform began to slide away and then stopped. Its brakes screeched. Cries and screams echoed again from the rear of the train.

"What's going on?" She panicked. "Danny what's wrong?" There was a crash of broken glass and more footsteps scurrying toward the stairs. A woman's screams. Yelling.

"I'm trying to see," I said peering around the corner and tensing my fingers along my side where my pistol would have once been. "I can't make it out," I repeated just as the crowd dispersed and the spectacle came in to view.

A group of men had smashed one of the train windows and pulled someone clean out through the glass. As soon as he had cleared it completely, the train roared off disappearing in a cloud of dust suspended in the air. The group surrounded the man and I considered stepping into help him.

"Don't go," she said, "Stay here and protect me." I found her hand on my arm, and that I had almost come around the corner. Only she held me back.

I looked at her and then back at the fighting. We could try to make the stairs. I could see the fear on her face like little fires stoking flames in her cheeks.

I sat down and put my arms around her.

"It will be all right. Shh," I said, "I'll protect you." I stroked her hair and she clung to me. We could hear the sounds of punching like slapping a slab of meat against a table and then whistles.

Piercing whistles shifted the strained mood of the station. Police swarmed. Twenty at least from the sound of their feet. I stroked her hair again and fought the urge to stand and look. The group cussed and complained, but they were taken away leaving the broken man behind.

After a moment we returned to our bags. I hid the blundering man from her and ushered her onto the train. We found our cabin easily while the passengers came to life laughing off the event like chatter in a theater.

"You were in the war, weren't you?" she said.

"Yes," I replied as I stored the bag over our heads.

"Why didn't you say something last night?" Cynthia's tone and manner grew serious and dark in a way that I didn't know how to approach.

"I don't know a man who didn't fight in it," when I discovered that I couldn't hold her defiant eyes, I looked out the window to conceal emotions that I didn't want to reflect upon.

"We really don't know that much about each other, do we?" she contemplated.

The door slid open and another couple joined us in the cabin. Cynthia reverted to her simple charm. The giddiness had left and been replaced by a calculated avoidance.

The issue would resurface that much I knew, but I couldn't prepare for it. I didn't know where she stood, yet I understood that she wasn't a fan of fighting and would think carefully about everything that she said.

* * *

We pulled away from the station and left the comfort and familiar mountain vista of Zurich behind for a new gallery of European delight.

The train's iron wheels rattled and roared while Cynthia chatted and again the cold grip of winters past settled in over my heart. I had only seen these hills in the light from the sky and had only travelled by train in the night.

We started high and the sun lit the green mountains like a sloped plain that bent out and away taking your eyes toward the open and rolling valley below and then up to the high tops of our mountain's further brothers glazed and shining with white under the sun which shook further out in the clouds burying this crystalline vision in your mind forever after.

Transfixed as I was, the vision broke with each tunnel we dove into and renewed with each valley we returned to. On each slope stood town and house above us and below us with sheep and cattle and goats. I watched them with suspended curiosity hoping that our destination might be like that little town on the tall hill far away that seemed to have no road to take any one to it or any of its people away.

Switzerland.

I understood it now in a way that I hadn't before even as a passenger on this very line. In some ways it reminded me of my little town far away in the Ohio River Valley, but in the sun here with that sparkling sheen that seemed to only cascade luminescent green through the Alps, I could not imagine any real darkness settling in over its men.

I saw distant kites or balloons and I had to turn away from the myriad of colors in the sky. I found a tear in my eye and wiped it away unsure as to why it was there and thankful that no one had seen.

In time Bern came into view and in many ways it came out from between the old mountains triumphant like a victorious statue, but one merely had to look at its cream-colored walls and feel the vibrant life permeating from its people.

"Why are we slowing?" Cynthia asked.

"I don't know," one of her new friends said. There was some ruckus and discussion. Cynthia did all the talking. She came back dejected and angry.

"The train has broken down. We must stay here in Bern tonight. They've given us vouchers."

"Oh, how wonderful. I've always wanted to be to Bern," the lady said. They reintroduced themselves to me as Veronica and Sam, but I kept forgetting who they were, so I brooded in my nostalgia and followed after Cynthia as she took our new friends to a hotel she hoped was still there.

We had become a rather strange party. Sam and Veronica were happy darlings lost in the clamor of the new love that Cynthia and I had shared only that morning, but now we were two strangers partaking in formalities with a new uncertainty hanging over our heads.

I hadn't noticed how much Cynthia had carried our side of the group until she had clammed up beneath the weight of whatever disappointment caused this change, and so while on the way to the hotel, I told the other two about my time in Japan after the war.

"Excuse me sir," Cynthia spoke in easy Swiss-German to the host. I caught every other word. "What do you mean there is only one room? That can't be possible. There's a kite festival this weekend? Acceptable? My friends here need a room. He's nah-ever mind that. We'll take the room." She took the key and turned sharply marching toward us.

"Veronica, Sam, there was only one room," she said. "It's an expensive hotel, and you're welcome to take the room for the night. We'd love to catch up for breakfast tomorrow."

"We really couldn't impose, but thank you. We plan to take the earlier train before the sun rises," they said and declined politely and left us with a forwarding address in Chicago. As soon as they were gone Cynthia relaxed.

"I couldn't stand them," she said, but I could still see the pallor in her face. Something else bothered her, but I shrugged off the urge to press in case it lingered from our morning adventure.

We, or I, took our bags up a narrow set of carpeted stairs and then down a long hallway with damask curtains and Spanish tapestries until we had come to the oak door at the back. Cynthia put the key in and turned.

It creaked open and then the luxuriousness of her life without me appeared. Silk sheets, polished brass banisters and all sorts of strange cosmetics. I had walked into a chemist's laboratory full of strange suffocating smells.

"Take a seat on the bed, will you? I'll just be a moment to freshen up and then we can go to dinner."

* * *

Cynthia woke me just as it was getting dark. A light drizzle forced us to walk beneath the covered walkways that line the streets and make the town like one enormous interconnected maze or mall whichever you prefer at the time. Cynthia had a sense of where we were going and intermittently the clock tower at the heart of Bern would come into view until we stood underneath its faint glow.

We walked through the center square until we found a restaurant with a covered patio. The place was deserted.

"Just a little rain and no one goes for dinner? The place last night was packed," I said.

"They are Europeans," she said coldly, "the crowd will pick up in a couple hours for the early crowd. They always know we're Americans, because we show up before six thirty."

I checked my watch. 6:05.

A waiter eventually came over and took our order. He complimented us on our exquisite taste as far as Americans are concerned. We had enough time to pick aperitifs, deserts, entrées and everything in between while we had been waiting, but our talk had died with the morning train.

I played with my napkin and then asked for a cup of black coffee. It was an Air Force habit, I told myself, because I didn't want to tell her, but I felt like she was judging my every action as if it was in some way geared for the moment when I plunged a sword or bullet into a surrendered foe.

Something was on her mind, but it didn't feel like the right time to ask it.

"How do you like Bern?" she asked.

"It's calm," I said, "Didn't see much on the ride in, but the square is nice."

"Just wait until you see it in the daylight," she said and looked across the square toward a large restaurant on the other end.

We finished dinner as some Swiss guests began to show up and then walked back to the hotel. The rain was done, but we still walked off the street. She tucked her hands away and existed entirely within herself.

I followed her along the streets until the buildings opened up and the ravine appeared beneath us. The houses stacked up on the mountains in the distance and the city followed the river around its meander.

Cynthia put her hands on the stone balcony. I did the same and watched her. She stared blankly out across the darkened valley.

"You know you can swim in the river if you like?"

We hovered there left inside of this difficult bubble to understand revolving around each other like celestial bodies in the sky unable to touch.

When we got to the hotel, I began stacking things on the floor. She looked at the gesture with a strange nonchalance. She neither remarked on my chivalry nor looked disappointed for my lack of aggression.

I wished I didn't care as much as I did, but I wanted to find her out. She wasn't playing along.

She got ready for bed and turned off the lamp after making sure that I had settled in.

"Oh, come off it, Daniel. Get in the damn bed!" She yelled at me and then she said, "I trust you not to pull any coup d'etat. The bed is a King and you've been the politest thing. What made you think I wanted you to take the floor?"

I settled in beside her without saying anything, but smiling to myself about an old joke that a friend of mine used to play on me when we bunked together in Southern Italy.

"Really, Daniel, please. What was it? We've come all this way from New York together and are sharing a room."

"You had that air about you like something was wrong. I thought it was about the war."

"No," she said but didn't continue.

"Something else then?"

"Yes."

I decided to shut up and we turned the light back off. I could feel her warmth radiating through the bedsheets and to me. I wanted to pull her close, but it wasn't the right moment. I supposed it may never be, but I didn't want to ruin the trip on the second evening.

She felt the same way I discovered shortly when she began to talk like grade school friends at a slumber party where we were the last two awake.

"What was the war like?" she asked.

"Awful," I chuckled, "No, it wasn't so bad, but it as. Both at the same time. Because of the people in my unit, I felt purpose. We shared the fear and the risk and the danger together, and somehow that made us all the more powerful like we could handle any amount of dark days."

"Were you afraid?"

"Always, but it was an afraid that you grew accustomed to and you knew that was what you fought to leave behind. To give your children a world without fear."

"That's kind of romantic of you, Danny," she turned over and looked at me. I glanced at her and smiled. I wondered if she could see the flash of my teeth in the dark.

"It's not so bad now that it's over."

"My dad died in Bern," she said and turned away again. "There I said it. That's why I've been acting so strange since we arrived. It didn't have anything to do with your damn war." I could hear her heave heavy sighs of relief.

"Are you okay?"

"I've never talked to anyone about it before."

"What about your mother?"

"Especially not her," she said and then sized me up, "and the first person I tell is the first man that I share a bed with."

"What happened?" I said astonished and pleasantly amused by both her candor and the sudden way she had held her breath. She was serious and upset. I could hear it in her voice. It lingered in the air and left a bowling ball where my stomach should have been.

"It was my eighth birthday and we came here as we always did for my birthday. He had a heart attack when we went down to the river to swim. The ambulance came, but it was too late to save him they said. They didn't even try. Anyway, it was many years ago and I don't know why it still upsets me so much, but it does."

"It's a big deal," I said.

"No it isn't. Not compared to," she stopped. "Goodnight Daniel."

"Goodnight. Cynthia. Sleep sweet."

Bell towers and the rain
Chapter 6

She woke me in the morning, fully dressed, with a determined look I hadn't seen on her before like we had to get out early to make it to all the rides at a theme park before anyone else.

We went out onto the street and it was the most perfect day with wispy clouds and the same sun as on the mountain train that lit up the green in the grass and trees.

"Come this way," she said and took my hand leading me down toward the ridge where we had stood the night before. There were men playing life-size chess that waved Hallo and we weaved our way through the garden and puppies to the stone balcony.

"It's beautiful," I said to her. The river sparkled below and I thought about what she had said yesterday. It was only a little warm. A perfect day for a swim, but no one was in the water yet this early in the morning.

"It is, isn't it?" She smiled happily and for a moment we stood there soaking in the view from the natural veranda. Finally Cynthia said, "I like coming to a place that I've been before, because I get to see it again."

"That's what usually happens," I chuckled and we turned away from the vista. She took my hand again and pulled me down the slope toward the bend in the river.

"You know. From a different perspective I mean. I feel like I've missed it all the first time or forgotten just how pretty it was."

Our promenade took us down Main Street and as the church, steeples, and smoke stacks receded toward the river, I could make out a bridge and a busying walkway up to an overlook outside the city.

"What's that up there? Is that where we are going?" I asked pointing to where the thin crowd in the lazy morning was heading. She pulled me close, rubbing her head against my shoulder and whispering in my ear.

"Be patient Danny, you'll see. Oh, what's this? Look at these paintings."

"They're nice," I nodded.

"Everyone is so good at everything these days. How could anyone get any better?"

"Hmm, maybe just new people come along and just do the same thing differently?"

"True, maybe. Take a look at this painter though. Doesn't it look just like Cezanne's?"

I chuckled at the innocent way she said it reminding me of one of my nieces.

"Quite a likeness, hah," I said, "Would you like to take a look inside? I think I'll grab something at this trinket shop here for my nieces."

"That's a nice idea. I'll go ahead and talk to him."

We separated for a moment. After I had picked out little Einstein heads I noticed a set of postcards at the clerk's counter.

"You know he lived here," the clerk said in English.

"Huh, I didn't know that actually," I said, "I know a few little girls that are huge fans of his."

"It's true. He lived just there across the street. Do you have a woman back home?"

"Only my sister," I said, "These are for my nieces."

"Don't forget a postcard."

That's right. I had to remember to write Mary before I left Bern. Between a sketch of the town with the church in center view compared to one with our morning view of the river's vale, I took the church one.

I paid in Swiss francs what seemed like a ridiculous amount, scribbled some lines on it, and stashed it my chest pocket. I met Cynthia again just as she came out of the painter's shop with an acute frown.

"Oh, I'm such a fool," she said.

"What? What did you say?"

"I told him that I liked the paintings."

"Sure you did. Cynthia, that hardly seems foolish."

"Well, then he asked me to buy one. Ruined the whole thing," she said.

"Can you blame him?"

"Can't I? I'd have bought one if all he cared about were the paintings."

"Fair enough."

While we were talking, we had neared the bridge across the crystal clear river. She asked about the little toy that I had picked up and then went silent for a moment. She gripped my hand tighter while we joined the loose pilgrimage of older couples dispersed along the path.

Then we were across the bridge and her mood brightened even further like a powerful beam of light had been subdued by this dark prism that stood before her heart until she had broken it at last.

She squeezed my hand once and then let go so that she could show me the little pen where Bern kept its brown bears. She pointed them out and told me what their names had been when she was last here. We took the pathway up the hill toward the overlook in comfortable silence.

I caught the whiff of a familiar scent and sniffed the air. She looked at me expectantly.

"It's one thing that I like about Switzerland. It always smells like flowers everywhere we go."

"That's because we are at the Rose Garden and they are just in bloom," she smiled. It was her grand reveal. Rose bushes lined our right and the full view of the city came up on our left as we climbed out from the stony path.

"Bern," she said and presented it.

"Huh," I said and pulled out the postcard. "That's where they got it."

She took the card and slapped my chest.

"Danny, you big fool, you've ruined it."

"What's that?" I asked, but she was already off and running through the park between a series of gazebos toward covered walkways.

I chased after. At first I walked briskly, but then I saw that she was giggling and wanted to see what all the fun was about. I lunged and almost caught her, but she ducked in between some gates at the last minute in a peel of laughter.

Wooden slates covered in green vines hid her from my view, but I could hear her giggling on just the other side.

"What is it that you want, Danny?"

"You Cynth," I said.

"Come and get me."

I stepped quickly around the corner and caught her in my arms.

"This is it?" she said.

"Wha--."

Her lips found mine.

"The moment when we first kiss."

I kissed her again. I lifted her up and twirled her in the green light that split through the vines that stretched along the slats of wood covering the walkway. Yellow and pink roses climbed the vines around us in a dazzling kaleidoscope array like swirling dye.

"I love you Cynthia Gold," I said startling myself.

"I love you too Daniel Kennig."

* * *

The rest of the day passed in a haze. We shopped the streets of Bern and turned in early to get ready for dinner. Cynthia was even more her usual self, jumping around the room and organizing as if time stood still for her.

I lay on the bed and watched her until she kicked me out, so that she could 'properly prepare'.

She told me to meet her at the Kornhauskeller at six so I walked around the square and dreamed of sketching the clock tower while watching someone paint it.

I took a seat on the fountain and let the day go easily by content now in having won the heart of a woman I admired greatly for her passion.

There was nothing else in life, save for maybe the love of God and country, as motivating, fear-inducing, and elating as that which I carried with me now in my soul like a bottled-up potion for power.

I went over the square to the Kornhauskeller early and discovered we would be dining once again in near complete solitude at the early end of the schedule. I asked for a table at the back under the great sandstone wall with a mural that looked like a pearlescent full moon.

I grabbed a menu and discovered I understood very little if any of the names in it. I knew them for Italian, but I couldn't place them easily.

I flagged the waiter and on the second try, he began to approach. I looked over his shoulder just as Cynthia left the staircase for the main floor. The balconies to the left and right framed her and the lighting bouncing off the painted stone lit up her skin like spotlights shining from beneath her.

My heart wrenched. I stood putting my hand on the chair beside me. My napkin fell to the floor. I tightened my jaw and smiled. A shiver ran down my spine.

"You look beautiful, Cynthia," I said stumbling over my words.

"Thank you Danny, but I didn't end-."

"You don't understand Cynthia. I think you are perfect right now."

She smiled and sat down, folding her hands, and silently smirking to herself again and again.

"One of the waiters said they would have some live music tonight," I said.

"That's odd," she looked around, "huh, it must be a nice venue." She trailed off looking around at the stone walls like she were evaluating the natural acoustic quality inherent in their design as a granary.

"I thought so too."

"Did they say who or what would be performing?"

"A singer with instrument accompaniment. I couldn't make out what he said it was exactly. I think it was a flute or something, but we'll see."

"That'll be nice. I guess you're right," she looked down at the menu and smirked again.

"I'm surprised Cynthia. I half expected something witty out of you about the whole thing."

"Witty?" she asked.

"You know deep and profound as you always are all the time."

"That's the problem with being deep and profound all the time," she said. "People come to expect it from you. Pretty soon you've used all your best stuff and you just end up seeming scatterbrained."

"Like Einstein," I said in passing thinking of the little toys I had picked up that morning.

"My father loved Einstein too," she said.

"Cynthia," I said, "I'm sorry I didn--."

"It's fine," her voice lit with happy memories, "he used to call me his little Einstein all the time. Part hopeful. Part proud. He pushed me to do my best."

"You do seem a lot like Einstein. You even sometimes have the hair," I joked, "and you sure are smart. Maybe the smartest person I've ever met."

"Yes, but sometimes all you want to talk about is the color of that girl's clothes and all the petty things you've missed by not judging any one on their ignorance."

"I'm all ears if you'd like to make up for lost time, now." I winked.

"You know that's why I like you so much Daniel. You accept me as who I am and don't try to put me in a box. I've spent my whole life listening to what I ought to be, what I ought to do, and how I ought to do it. Men. Women. Strangers and friends. I am not a mannequin. I am not a pigeon or a doll. I am a grown woman."

"I can tell you one thing," I said as the wine finally came, "You're certainly not alone in that."

"Are you ready to order?" the waiter asked, his accent suddenly so much more French than German that it was startling, "Oh, you haven't looked at ze menu. I will return."

"If you could help me with the menu, I would be delighted," I said and so for a moment our conversation turned to food. Risottos and capreses. We ate and drank well and the restaurant gradually filled in around us.

"What do you want, Danny?" Cynthia asked after we clinked glasses for at least the third toast to Bern and Switzerland or Bern and Einstein.

"Haven't I told you?"

She shook her head and drank some more, "You've been purposely coy."

"Have I?" I lifted my glass, stuck my nose in like she showed me and twirled it then said, "You've asked it enough certainly. Don't you remember?"

"Something good to happen. Me."

"Those aren't good enough answers?"

"I mean what do want Danny? Like really want."

"Out of life?"

"Out of life. Out of everything. Out of your career? I don't even know what your career is."

I acted like I was taking my time chewing a piece of tender steak.

"I can see it in your eyes like firecrackers or like when you tell children about the man in the moon."

"All right, Cynthia."

"Why can't you tell me?"

"I am telling you. All right?" I said. She nodded. "I am a singer and I want to be great. Better

than great. I want to be the best singer there ever
was. When you think of singers, I want you to think
of me first and then everybody else. I want my name
up in lights. I want the world on a string."

She grinned, "Will I get to hear you sing?"

"Someday."

"Now?"

"Isn't that the way it always goes, isn't it?"

A trill rose up through the rafters like a siren.
The room went dead.

We hadn't noticed how loud it had become
until the air had gone out and suddenly we could
hear it raining outside like a waterfall.

A beautiful flute solo shocked us into
suspended animation. Everything from before stayed
right where it was. Even the waiters hovered in place
wondering if there was some cue for them to return
to their tables.

Everyone clapped when it ended. Many wiped
tears from their eyes and some stood.

"I apologize, my friends," the little French
flutist told the crowd. "My partner. The singer
Cherie Le Blume has grown sick with the spring air
and so that will be our performance for the evening."

"Wait," Cynthia said and got up, "My
husband's a singer."

"Your husband?" the flutist replied.

"Yes. We're from America. We're well known in New York. Could you do a performance with him?"

"Oh ho. New York. Oui, oui. I could do a performance with a man from New York."

I could feel my skin burn hot and red like a radish as the French flutist mocked me with a snide smile and a hearty wink. I bet to myself that he was thinking this poor American chap would fall straight on his face.

"Of course if monsieur is not up for it."

"I am certainly plenty up for it," I said putting my napkin down on the table and standing up tall like I was prepared to salute. "Do you know Nacio Herb Brown?"

He nodded.

"Man of Manhattan from Ziegfeld Girl?"

He nodded. I drank the last of my wine and surveyed the audience like a hunter.

With a wink, I said, "Sit down darling. I've got one song to sing, and I'm singing it for you." I moved out and away from the table. The flutist with his mocking eyes began on a low note and then took a paradiddle into a crescendo. When he dropped, I began to sing with his harmony.

It can be lonely to be
a Man of Manhattan.
Don't get me wrong, I can see
the way they swoon when I pass them,
but when they come, they often go

and I've been left on my own.

But here you are and I know.
Tonight, I've got a chance
to have my last first dance.
Tonight, I've met a girl
with a fire in her heart,
and you know, I'm telling all the world.

She's a pretty little dancer
with a grin I can't believe.
She's as witty as a fox
and her voice just makes me dream.

Tonight, I've got a chance
to have my last first dance at last.
Tonight, I've found a girl,
and she's taken my heart with her.
Tonight, we show the world what it means
to live at the center of it all.

We'll bring the swing back to the streets,
and have pianos dueling to the beat.
She wants to salsa in the square
and everywhere we go, we're singing to the air.

The applause was deafening. It echoed
throughout the stone building and came from the
balconies and the crevices. Every diner had turned
around to see who it was that sang so sweetly.

Cynthia looked at me with another coy smirk telling me I'd done it now Danny.

I bowed. The flutist came and congratulated me. Many others came to shake my hand. He apologized for having doubted me and clapped his hand on my back.

I signaled for us to leave. Cynthia took care of things, reorganizing the crowd and negotiating the check. The restaurant refused to take our money, so she stuffed a hundred francs or so in the chest pocket of the manager and we ducked into the rain together despite many objections.

"Oh, Danny, you're the best there ever was," she laughed as we went toward the clock tower in the square.

We ran back under the walkway already soaked.

"You really think so?" I asked.

"Oh Danny, you're too much fun. What am I going to do with you?"

She stood on the edge of the pounding rain, where it bounced up off the street and onto her dress like a curtain of grey beads. I went to grab her and she jumped into the rain laughing.

I jumped in after her and we ran through the rain as it poured over us. I caught her at the fountain.

"Well, now that you've got me, Mr. Kennig," she said, "What are you going to do with me?"

I put my lips to hers and we kissed. I ran my tongue along her wet chin, nuzzled against her and then whispered into her ear.

"I want you Cynthia."

She pulled away to slap me playfully. She rubbed my chest where she had hit me and bit her lip.

We were together in the hotel. I had no memory of the time between but for the taste of her lips on my tongue and the vaguely heavy feeling with which I felt lost within.

In the elevator she wrapped herself around me.

"They asked me today if I still wanted a second room," she said. I shifted myself to be between her legs and she nuzzled her forehead into my chest, "I told them we would only be needing the one."

We kissed eagerly in the hallway and she pulled me into the bedroom. The water dripped after us and when we got into the room we sunk into the plush carpet.

"No, I'm too wet, Danny, let me dry off in the washroom."

"I don't mind," I took her body in my arms again and pulled her near.

"Mmm," she pressed against me as we kissed. I could feel her heart throb against my chest. "No."

She pushed herself away and into the bathroom while I took off my clothes and laid them out on the windowsill. I peered through the blinds at the beautiful night and saw the church's bell tower lit up in the distance.

"Danny?"

"Yes dear?"

"Could you help me with this quickly?"

"What is it, darling?"

"The zipper on the back of my dress. I can't get it. It's stuck."

I followed her voice into the bathroom. She sat on the edge of the tub playing with her hair. She had a comb or a file in her mouth and twisted her hair wringing it out. Gushing water poured out onto the tub floor.

"That's better," she sighed, rubbing her neck and stretching it. "As stupid as this sounds, could you help me with this?" She indicated her zipper.

I sat on the tub ledge beside her and eased her out of the slim dress following the silver trail with my lips from just where her hands had been.

Her back arched and she purred, but then caught my hand, "God, I'm tired. What time is it? I feel like we've been out all night."

"Not even nine," I said showing her my pilot's watch. "Looks like time is on our side."

"All right, Mr. Einstein," she joked.

Cynthia wrung more water out of her hair and let it fall to her back where my hands dug slow circles into her bare shoulders. She looked back and up at me. When I smiled at her, her pupils dilated and I went in to taste her lips.

She put a finger to my chin and then grabbed my jaw with the other, "What have you seen?" She peered into my soul, her eyes shaking as they searched from eye to eye. "What darkness out there? Or in here now?" She touched my heart.

"I can't tell you Cynthia."

We sat there in silence for what felt like an eternity suspended beneath the flickering dim light of the bathroom lamp with the constant drip from her hair falling onto the edge of the tub.

"Not tonight," she said and pushed me away.

* * *

I woke up early the next morning refreshed just as the sun broke through a crack in the blinds. I turned to my right to find the bed empty. On the pillow was a letter.

"I'm out in the Dahlholzli Park. When you're done catching up on your time, Mr. Einstein, would you care to join me by the River Aare? -Cynthia. P.S. I'll be back before ten if you wake up too late."

Forever playful. I dressed quickly, asked for some directions and set out on the street. The Kirchenfeldbrucke road led me over the water on a pretty bridge. It took me past a few statues and museums and then down a long street to a thick wood in the city. I took the first gate in and the sun was gone.

The thick canopy coupled with the heavy rain from the night before created a murky wood that was more like going into Appalachia than Central Park. The woods were vibrant in that way that nature comes alive in the day after a rain storm. The damp air hung like a light mist and the birds chirped between the sounds of the trees shaking in the morning wind. Droplets of water sprayed over me.

The wind tore through the trees angrily sending an unnerving chill up my spine. I felt watched even though there was no one around. The forest grew deep and wide as I followed the beaten dirt pathway further away from Bern.

Alone on my walk and without the aid of the sun, in the murky mist, surrounded by the sounds of the wild feasting on what the rain had kicked up in the dirt, the hair on the back of my neck began to stand on end. I clenched and unclenched my fists and worried whether Cynthia was okay.

Were there wolves in these woods? I wondered and then broke into a slight job agitated by the reception that I received from the old forest.

There was nothing wrong with a forest. Only this one stood remote, different, and mysterious. Unfamiliar corners hid behind the mist that hung in the heavy air. The angry noises possessed a defensive, almost accusing tone. Who was I to have entered their forbidden garden, they said.

The path forked ahead and the path to the right darkened when the sun went behind some clouds. I took a left and followed a long bend until I came around on a long path that ran farther into the distance than I could see.

My breath caught in my throat. At least a hundred ravens lined the middle of the path. They croaked and flapped surrounding something in the middle of the road. Their heads turned in a jolt setting singular purplish black eyes like marbles on me with cold inquisitiveness.

My mind went blank. Cynthia? No, whatever the carrion feeders feasted upon looked too small to be human. I stood there for a moment wondering what the reason was that they were called a murder or was that the crow? Was there a difference? Would a murder of crows or ravens kill me quicker?

There were more. To the right and left black ravens perched on fallen trees near the path like spectator benches. A stump on either side marked their forest arena like gates into the netherworld.

A long rolling wind sang forth from the forest behind me and whispered as it passed deeper down the dirt road. The ravens swung up into it and cleared the path forward. The unfortunate small life that the birds picked at was unrecognizable.

"I trust you," I said to what I didn't know and proceeded through the gates marking nature's natural defensive barrier like passing into a secret circle.

The ravens stared unmoving. The woods opened and my head swam into the point where everything became full color and I only the passenger in the same way it did when the flak had shaken our bomber over Bologna. The mist that hung in the air distributed around me dispersing in the nearness but clouding out the distance.

"Thank you," I said and walked steadily. The ravens were behind me. I didn't look back.

At a trident in the road, I looked up at the trees and whispered, "Where do I go now?" The wind quietly turned through the trees and pulled me to the middle path and so I took it and slowed into an easy walking pace that I hadn't enjoyed since before moving to New York.

A jogger passed me and I smiled thinking that he too must have passed through the gates protected by whatever higher power existed in this bright wood.

At the end of the long bending path, the sun lit the edge of the forest like the end of a train tunnel too brilliantly to see what stood there. A figure formed as I neared bathed in the light as if radiating it outward and into the park behind me.

"There you are," Cynthia said.

The wind came behind me and I could hear it in the trees, but it was quieter now and indistinct having delivered me to my destination.

"I wondered if you'd be up early enough to catch me out here," she said.

"How was your morning walk?" I asked.

"Uneventful," she said. "It's nice to see that the forest is still here. I used to come here as a little girl. Come, take my hand, I'd like to show you the Eichholz camp grounds on the other side of the Aare."

We walked chatting intermittently. The forest stood tall to our right and the river ran along our left. We took a bridge across it and then walked back the direction that we had come toward Eichholz and away from Bern.

On this chilly spring morning, we had the small water front walk alone except for a few friendly elderly couples coming back from Eichholz. They waved at us and gave happy, loud guten morgens and bonjours at the same time wanting to make sure they welcomed us.

We were all people of Bern walking like bears along the river through the forest sanctuary. Cynthia sighed deeply and nestled her head against my shoulder, relaxing in the hopeful rising sun.

Peaceful as it was when we came to Eichholz, I realized why Cynthia had been reserved on our walk together. There was a small shoreline and a place to bathe in the water.

I didn't have to ask because she told me outright.

"This is where we used to come as a family to swim when we stayed in Bern," she said. I listened, holding my breath to let her speak her peace and get this heavy burden off her chest forever and for good. "It was here that we were coming to on the day my father died."

She tried to remain level and cool in the moment, but I could see tears well in her eyes despite the stillness of her lips. When I hugged her, she sobbed once and then let a couple more gasps of breath escape her before she regained her incredible composure.

"Let's go for a swim," I said prompting her to sniffle and wipe away her tears.

"I'm hardly dressed for--."

"Nonsense," I said looking around, "What is it? Half past eight? There's hardly anyone here."

I stripped off my shirt and pants and went into the cold water quickly and immediately regretting the decision. She put her hand to her chin and had a mischievous little laugh in her eyes.

"Come now, you can strip to your knickers if you don't want to swim in the nude and wear your dress over your nakedness until we get back to the hotel."

"Wouldn't you like that, Danny? You cad," she snorted with a burst of laughter as I grimaced in the cold water. "Look at you. You'll freeze to death."

"Nonsense, the water is fine," I could barely control the rattling of my teeth but I did.

"It's freezing," she said more adamantly this time. I swam further out into the river and under the sun. She watched with gazelle-like eyes as my arms turned in wide arcs like wheels in the shape of swan's necks.

"Fine," she said and with a look around she stripped down exposing even her breasts. Her body hardened in the chilly air, standing in the shade. She tiptoed into the river and I rose from the water to pull her in like an alligator.

In the river, lit by the sun, she warmed and we were together then swimming and she began to play pushing water at me and giggling.

I swam around her blasts and tackled her. She laughed harder and then in my embrace she quieted and looked at me again this time with tears in her eyes.

"Why are you so good to me, Mr. Kennig?" she asked.

"What do you mean?"

"You know what I mean."

"I love you Cynthia."

"You barely know me," she said. Her last bit of hesitance to trust showed. The final resistance surfaced and so I fought the urge to laugh.

"I know enough about you to know that you're too good to let walk away." Before she could speak I kissed her again on the lips and then on her wet eyelids dripping small bits of water from her eyelashes.

"Will you marry me Daniel Kennig?"

"Yes," I said wondering idly if she was serious but knowing in all reality that she was.

* * *

We spent a few weeks touring together, but there was an ultimate certainty now to the relationship. We were now completely a thing. Inseparable at all junctions. Our decisions merged into one, but there was a definite destination to our wandering.

London and her family obligations. Under her trust's rules, we would need to request the approval of her mother.

London Bound
Chapter 7

Marcus picked up the last letter. Daniel had sent such youthful hop in the last letter to Mary. The couple's romantic European adventure had come to an end and Marcus felt like he had helped send these young lovers on their way as if they had just departed on a tremendous voyage.

I had to put the letter down. I was shaking with how much anxiety suddenly coursed through my body. It felt like that time my team had lost the championship game. Would I have to take a cold shower just to calm down again?

I looked at my hands wondering at how my lips felt numb. I paced the study. I couldn't leave the room like this. I looked at the letter again wondering if I had misread it, but it was as plain as day. I rubbed my mouth and decided to get a glass of orange juice from the kitchen.

Mary, I'll be back in Indiana in a week. Cynthia called off the wedding. It's bad. Let me give you the details here just to get it off my chest, but just so you know it is both all my fault and impossible to go back. It is a matter of both political and religious opinion. The two things in my life that I can never imagine compromising on.

And so it's over.

Now, let me begin...

"Daddy, are you done with your working?" Allison asked.

I had walked into the kitchen on zombie mode and found myself scrounging for orange juice in the fridge when she walked up behind me.

"Daddy?"

"Hey there sweet cheeks. No, there's more to read, but I think I'm done for the night."

"Daddy?"

"What's up sweetie?"

"Are you okay?"

"What? Oh, egg beaters? How'd that get there? That would be gross, wouldn't it?"

Allison went to the fridge and worked the orange juice out of the door like she was pulling a sword from a stone. She leaned back as she threw the carton onto the counter with my help of course.

"There you go."

"Thank you," I chuckled having been grounded again in reality and welcoming the change in pace. It couldn't be the perfect romance forever, could it? Bern, Marseille, Florence, Valencia, Paris. Most of the stories had been small snippets with great expectations. Then, to just end. Certainly there was an explanation in there, but hadn't the couple been married? I had thought.

"What are you thinking about daddy?" Allison asked me. She was holding onto a teddy bear and looking up at me. God, she was so damn tiny I felt like papa bear being asked why I was worried about the storms of her future.

"Nothing, sweetheart."

"Were you thinking about the story you were reading?"

"Yes," I admitted, "I am reading ab-thinking about the story I was reading."

"Did something bad happen?" She was kind of rocking back and forth with nervous energy. Damn, she was a perceptive little shit. I wondered if anything I did got by her or if feeling like she hadn't noticed me picking my nose was as ridiculous as hoping she didn't hear me say fuck when the car door closed on my finger the other day.

"Yes, something bad happened."

"Awe," she said in an exaggerated tone like one of her favorite cartoon characters and twirled in a circle, "Do you want to read me a bed time story?"

"Do I want to?"

"Yeah!"

"Where's mommy?" I asked.

"I want you to read me a bed time story!"

"Okay," I complied, "but where's mommy?"

"She's in your guys's room."

"K, I will go check in on her and then be right back."

"No, daddy," she whispered now, "mommy is angry. Read me a story please." She had her puppy eyes now and I had to agree that I didn't want to deal with Shawna angry at the moment either.

"Fine, meet me in your room."

"No!"

"What?"

"Come with me," she said all serious and posturing like she was going to light on fire like the human torch.

"Okay, okay. What do you want me to read?"

"Will you read me the rest of your story?"

"I don't thin-."

"I won't be scared I promise."

"It's not that kind of story."

"What kind of story is it?"

"A love story."

"Did they get to a kissing part? You can skip those parts. They're gross."

"Okay, let me catch you up a bit and then if there are any bad parts, I will stop reading okay?"

"Yay!"

I would never get tired of that big smile on her face and that silly yay she would yell. I wished I could bottle the emotion up and hold it in my arms forever. She ran off and then came back immediately wary that I might change my mind. She followed me suspiciously to the study like a jailer accompanying me to my cell.

We went to her room and I began again the tale of Daniel Kennig, the greatest American singer, and Cynthia Gold, the woman of his dreams then and now.

* * *

Seeing the roof of the cherry house again appear from between the trees solidified the sense of impending dread that had clung to me since we took to the air in Paris. Home neared and so did my mother, Winifred, and whatever terror, horror, or jealousy lurked in her mind.

There was that and something about being in a plane with Daniel that had planted and hardened in my heart an ugly seed. He had tried to help when we landed but had grown tired of one word answers.

Luckily, the limousine driver kindly ignored the ill-tempered air. Had it been George who had arrived to take us from the airport, I don't know what I would have done.

In the long drive and short flight, with the solemn silence, I had been able to reconcile my thoughts from the most recent "whirlwind of the bizarre" as Devlin liked to call my worldly jaunts. And, it dawned on me in quite inexplicable ridiculousness that Daniel and I had met only two months ago in New York.

Two months and I had told him I'd loved him. I thought about Bern and the way it had felt like time had stopped for a short while to let us have a moment to ourselves. In the gaps between spaces all that was strange disappeared and the universe became friendly and familiar.

Now, although it may have felt like eons had passed since George and I had pulled around the fountain after driving down this very road, I was confronted by the very clear reality that it had barely been a month.

What would I tell mother? I wanted to run away from it all and ease back into our time that was, but it was gone now. We were always leading toward this and in all seriousness I felt as if this was the original inspiration for unstoppable force meets immovable object.

What would mother think?

My mind swirled around the obstacles that lie in wait like rocks along the shore. I felt Daniel, a strong comforting presence, sitting there beside me. At the same time I felt like a ball on a string. Rather than having sunk roots into the earth, I had found a light that burned bright and hot.

I couldn't dwell on it any longer. The car had stopped at the gate. Me and my soldier returning home. *Oh my God, what have I done?*

The limo driver handled the gate.

I wanted to skip this part, but I couldn't. We were here together for a reason. The old house looked for a moment like a stranger and then it set in that I was the one who had gone and come back changed.

Things had come between us. Big things, little things. Life had happened while I was gone.

New York and the rest of it.

I looked at Daniel.

He smiled. There it was. The warmth again came on easy as if it had never left and I became determined to stand up to my mother like I had never done before. All that I needed to know was that I had him.

If the drive up hadn't attracted the attention of the house, then the sound of the doors snapping open would have. I came up with a simple plan and with the renewed confidence popped out of the car.

Daniel followed suit. I could see that the energy infected him quickly.

"Daniel, attend to the bags with the driver. Could you?" I said and turned toward the front of the car, "Jon, was it? Jon, could you please wait outside for a moment with Daniel? I will just be in and back."

The old man, firm, gracious, and respectable, with a thick, trimmed, and fully white beard nodded and walked along the outside of the car with the stiff limp of a man who had lost full range of motion in the use of his legs.

The first Great War, I wondered, and thought about the types of things that my Daniel and a limo driver shared that could only be gained in the fog of war.

Daniel glanced up and his smile pulled off the last bit of ice that had solidified on the flight from Paris. I harnessed the love in the air, the warmth in the late spring air, and rushed into the house.

"Mother!" I yelled and repeated it around the foyer, up the stairs, and into the kitchen. I heard something around a corner and ducked through the door to the drawing room, "Mother? Oh, Mr. Kent."

"You're back?" he said. There was no warmth or smile in his voice. He looked put off and distant.

"Yes," I said. "Why, are you surprised?" We stood there in silence. He holding some cord for a lamp or something that he was helping to repair. Me in my one of my best dresses, kept tidy despite the cross-chanel flight.

"Is he here?"

"Who?"

"Cynthia, don't do this to me, of all people."

"What?"

"You know who." He looked at me with a muted and building anger seeping through his typically stoic resolve, "We got a letter post-marked from Manhattan just after you left to France from one Daniel Kennig of Prince Street."

"Daniel?" I played with my hair, "Yes, he is outside."

Mr. Kent grabbed my hand, "So, it's not official?"

"What isn't?" I shot my hand back and took a step toward the doorway.

"Cynthia, you foolish girl," he tisked, "We thought you had run off to elope with some sweetheart from New York."

Words formed in my head, but didn't make it all the way to my mouth before I lost them in my surprised stupor.

"At least you were smart enough to bring him here before making such a rash decision. Is he outside?"

I nodded.

"I'll inform the others."

"Where's mother?" I finally stammered, regaining a bit of what energy I had captured on the front stoop.

"She's in Bath for the weekend?"

"When will she be back?" I asked while following Mr. Kent to the door. "Is Mrs. Tabernathy out? I didn't see her in the kitchen."

"Cynthia, did you think that you would go and leave and life wouldn't go on while you were gone? Your mother has gone to Bath on the weekend for years. Most of the staff has off when you and your mother are out. Come. I'll see that he is put comfortably in one of the guest rooms."

We walked to the door. Mr. Kent found a decorative bowl to hide the cord he carried inside and he went out to greet Daniel with an adroit politeness that I could see Daniel read as genuine novelty.

In some ways it was, but I also felt sorry for good Midwestern Daniel. How could he know how to stop the staff of the house from plotting his downfall if he couldn't tell that the pleasure in Mr. Kent's voice was as false as the stucco marble paneling in some Parisian restaurants?

A strange defensive feeling came over me and extended outward to Daniel. I turned back inside. New, emotional traps had been set against me.

The shadows grew deep and wide. Everywhere I looked dark thoughts and questions lurked.

I saw a picture of my regal father posed for a photo in the twenties. Little of Daniel lived up to the richness in his dress or bearing.

I could not fight alone against my childhood home, but I could figure something out. I searched the study and found a pen emblazoned in gold with the name of his home state, Michigan. My father was proud of his roots despite the humble origins compared to the old money men that my mother led him toward later in life.

I jotted in clean and sharp blue.

Devlin, tea for two tomorrow at noon?

I scratched out two and wrote three. I wrote it over on a new sheet and took a deep breath.

* * *

The tea set clinked and I coughed.

"So," Devlin attempted to start up a conversation after the introductions had dissipated into awkward silence faster than my passionate plea for our love had dissipated the day before. My hapless charge had been wasted on the front steps, the foyer, and the hallways of the old house.

Now, with this whole fiasco over breakfast scones, Mrs. Tabernathy's disapproving looks, and the overbearing coldness of Mr. Kent, I finally realized just how difficult it would be to bridge the space between our two worlds.

Daniel Kennig, the soldier, sat with perfect posture on the hard edge of the chair at the head of the low table, but he had the manners of a country gentleman without an ounce of experienced decorum.

"Cynthia told me a little about you. You like to read and you're well-traveled."

Daniel drank some tea and then looked up at Devlin, "Were you asking a question?"

I gripped my saucer tighter and made sure my tea wasn't shaking by looking at the water.

"I guess not," said Devlin, "Did you attend university in the States?"

"No, I did not. I fought in the war."

"I understand with the war. You had a draft, but I know we had rotations. You weren't fighting all the time, were you?"

Daniel smiled and what I thought I might have once taken as an easy charm seemed now like harsh pity for the way in which Devlin skirted around the issue. We saw it as a matter of respect.

"I fought all the way through. Signed up before I turned eighteen by falsifying my certificates."

"Fascinating," Devlin said, "If you don't mind me asking, what did you do? You know with all the soldiering. I don't know much about it, but I find it incredibly interesting."

"I was an Air Force major on the Italian front," Daniel answered and as he began to answer in brief snippets about his exposure to the front line as an officer I recognized how little that he had talked about the war with me.

It was like he had set it off outside of him as something he had done in a dream. Now, I could see a change in his voice and manner that made me worry.

"Miss Gold, your scones are ready," Elizabeth knocked and brought the scones in.

"Finally, breakfast," Daniel seemed to be trying to lighten the mood, but I noticed Daniel regard

Elizabeth as she came in and left the tray. It made me a little furious with Devlin and me sitting right there.

"I didn't realize that I wouldn't be allowed to dust off my cook's skills. Oh, these are excellent. I can see why we were meant to wait for Mrs. Tabearnithy, was it? She's exceptional. Truly exceptional."

I covered my mouth slightly appalled at the way that he talked with food in his mouth still and didn't have the decency to cover it as he spoke.

"Try them," Daniel said. We ate with him. "I wonder if they are any good dipped in tea." I looked at Devlin and he had this strange grin that made me feel like he was watching an animal eat steak at the zoo.

"Major Kennig," Devlin said, "Let's talk about New York. I've only visited Cynthia once. I was thinking of making a trip there in July or August."

"September or October are much better."

"I could do both."

"Well, in that case, why wait?" Daniel's face lit up as he and Devlin started to chat about the city. Devlin had only been to posh places, and Daniel was suggesting the strangest little dives.

Elizabeth knocked on the door, "Miss Gold. There is a gentleman at the door to see you."

I turned and instinctively said, "Tell him to wait a moment in the foyer, I'll be right there."

Daniel looked at me with a suspicious, hurt glance, "Would you rather him come by later?" It seemed less of a suggestion than a demand.

"You two boys are having quite enough fun without me. I feel like you can handle yourselves."

I put down my tea and was in the process of adjusting my dress skirt to stand up when Daniel stood first.

"Is this the door to the backyard? I feel like I need a little air."

"Yes," Devlin said, "Let me show you."

They went out one direction and I the other. Fitzwilliam stood in the foyer dressed handsomely with that same rigid military posture, but none of the bad habits picked up from life among common men. I could see now what my mother had looked for. She wanted someone who fit into our London circle.

I smiled.

"You look upset," Fitzwilliam said, "Should I come back? Did you have company over?"

"No, yes," I said, stumbling over my words, "I'm glad you've come."

"I had heard you were in town, and."

"I meant to send you a letter," I said, "But I only returned yesterday evening."

"It seems I've been outed. I've been keeping too close a watch," he bowed slightly, "I came to reaffirm my intention to take you to the Summer ball."

"I," I looked at his hopeful eyes, but I knew what my answer must be, "I can't."

"You can't?" The disappointment surged up quickly and I could see his face burst with redness and tears form at the corners of his eyes.

"I mean, I don't know if I will be in town for it and."

"It's less than a week away."

I held my tongue for a moment, wondering what mother might say about Daniel. What would happen in the next few days? I felt so out of sorts already.

"Could I beg you to reconsider?" he asked.

"Yes, that's fine," I felt control slipping from me. What was I to do? Here was a man that fit into my world, but I had loved another. I still loved another, but he hadn't lasted a day without showing his colors.

"Will you write me a letter? Should I stop by again?"

"Yes," I said. Trying to find somewhere to look as my eyelids grew heavy and my hands grew numb, "Yes, I'll write. Let me think. About it."

"Should I stay for tea?"

"I have girlfriends over," I lied. I wasn't quite sure why I didn't just tell him the truth, but of course he had to leave, "I'll write you."

"I will anxiously await your response. Take care Lady Cynthia." He bowed and exited.

"Take care Fitzwilliam," I said and found myself pulling myself back together slowly as I drifted into the space where the tea set had been arranged.

He was so splendid in his full white suit like a little toy soldier, but he hadn't fought in the war. Not directly. Oh, what a mess I had gotten myself into now.

I collapsed into the chair.

Devlin and Daniel returned. They came with the smell of cigarettes on their lips, and my stomach might have twisted in a gymnast's knot.

"You smoke?" I asked. "Every time I think I know you, I find I don't." I stormed out of the room before he could respond. Had I missed some comment of his in Paris?

I wanted to see Mrs. Tabernathy in the kitchen. Maybe she would have some pearl of wisdom. Of course, I couldn't be too forthright with her, because she was against Daniel and me as well.

Now, I had to fight the urge to run into the study, lock the door, and be with my dad's things.

None of it had gone according to plan.

I was disappointed in myself. Yes, of course, but I was also disappointed in Daniel.

* * *

We sat in the patio chairs with Daniel. He to my left and mother across from me. A pitcher of English iced lemon tea perspired at the middle of the table.

It was up to him now. He alone would have to win over my mother. If he could attain her blessing, then my doubts would be squelched.

His charm had come alive. Mum looked pleasantly surprised by the way in which he had introduced himself and complimented both her and me. I wondered if he had taken some pointers from Devlin, gentleman extraordinaire.

"I must say when I found out that Cynthia was meeting an American man in France. I thought the worst, but you are really a pleasant surprise."

"Mother, you did marry father."

"In France?" Daniel asked. Thankfully mother brushed him off.

"Or wherever, but that was different sweetheart."

"How was that different?" I asked.

"Your father was a. A gentleman of," she said, "certain qualification."

"And how do you know Daniel isn't the same?"

"Quite," mother said, "Well, Daniel, then what is it that you do?"

"I'm a singer for one of the clubs in New York."

"One of the big ones?" mother asked. "Like the Carnegie."

"It doesn't quite work like that," he replied.

"No matter," she waved her hand over it as if brushing away a fly along with the semantics, "So, but, you're a good singer though of course? That's why my Cynthia here, likes you. She met you at some event or some other."

"He's an excellent singer."

"Actually we met at a café near Union--"

"Daniel," I tried to hint to him subtly that some things were best left out altogether.

"--Square."

"Really? I suppose it's a nice area. If you're a singer, then, would you care to sing us a song?"

"No one ever takes you at your word anymore," he chuckled, "You always have to prove it until they chase your coattails. I apologize I'm not feeling it at the moment."

"Oh, come now. You don't have people chasing at your coattails now? Look at you. There's Cynthia. One song, even not at your best should be fine."

"He really is a terrific singer," I said. "Daniel, could you?"

He shook his head, "I'm sorry. It is not a talent that is always on demand."

"Well, you have to do so many shows, don't you?" Mother asked.

"Yes, we do, but we get plenty of time to rehearse."

"You know in my youth it was the women who learned to entertain. I remember practicing five hours a day. The piano, mind you. To make sure I could properly play Claire de Lune or Fleur de Lys on demand for my future husband. You didn't get the choice to perform or not."

"Huh, I'm sorry, Mrs. Gold, I feel like my voice has been caught in my throat. Another time."

I clenched my hands together and hoped that the conversation would take a better turn. I felt like it must have been the cigarettes, because he seemed confident enough.

"Oh all right, if you don't feel up to it," she sighed, "At least Kennig. Did you grow up in the New York area?"

"Indiana."

"Notre Dame is around there. I would hear of it from my husband ceaselessly. You must be an Irish Catholic then?"

"Protestant."

"Whoever heard of an Irish Protestant from America?" Mother practically gasped and she looked at me like I was crazy with the thoughts being practically forced into me. *Did you know that you had invited a Protestant into our home!*

"Well, I have heard of an Irish Protestant. As I am one," he smiled.

"You must enjoy New York though. I've heard. Indiana is in the Midwest, right? I've heard that the Midwest, but particularly Indiana and Ohio can be dreadfully conservative. They even voted Republican this past time, right?"

Daniel's face was bright red, "I'm a Republican. I voted Republican and I will continue to do so."

"Oh, that's simply. How can you go about lauding that with all that war mongering?"

"Mother."

"The Democrats brought us into the most recent war. Besides, I fought in the war, and I was glad to do so for my country and for freedom."

"Daniel, please."

"Well, you were pressed into it. The Democrats are hardly to blame, but the social programs were really something spectacular. I've been mentioning them among my friends in the Parliament."

I tried to interject again, but they ignored me. I folded my arms and watched it all unfold like a car crash in the snow. Each car drifting lazily toward each other stubbornly unable to change course.

"One step toward Socialism I say."

"Oh poo. How do you expect to get anything done then?"

"Through responsible programs and measures fit to their time."

"I don't think we can have this conversation. You seem completely uninformed."

"I do?" Daniel said.

"Yes."

"You aren't even in America or from there."

"All the better to evaluate it with a more astute eye. Republicans are nothing but backwater ingrates who as far as I am concerned don't read."

"And you know so much more than we do?"

"The world is desperate for our opinion."

"Your opinion? You sit here hidden away, pretending to care, and voicing the most liberal positions. Do you think anyone wants to know what you think? Do you think anyone cares?"

"Oh but they do. You think the world would go and become better off and forget about us? The old money forgotten by the new? No, we're more important than ever before, because they are just learning about what we've always had. Now, they're hungry. They want validation. And voila, they've discovered us anew. And in us, in viewing our actions, in every similarity they may see some paragon in themselves whether or not it's there. We've become their guides."

"Guides? Do you think you're above God?"

"Well," mother shrugged. "It is the only approval they seek."

Daniel threw his napkin down, "That's enough. I've heard enough." His voice soared into the one that he used when he had sung at the Kornhauskeller and boomed her into a stunned silence, "I am proud of Indiana. There are good people there who have decency, integrity, and grace. Just as I hope that your husband is or was proud of his home state, and I don't think it is a badge of courage or power, to be a piece of shit whether you use pretty language or not. It's a disgrace."

He turned and went in through the door to the back hall and I followed after him.

"Daniel? Daniel. Daniel!" I caught him by the arm.

"You were right Cynthia. I was not prepared for your mother, and I can see why you were worried about coming here. We can go together. Back to New York."

"Daniel."

"I'm not some toy to be wound up to sing."

"I happen to believe a lot of the same things that my mother believes."

"If we can go to New York together--." He grabbed me by the shoulders and pleaded into my eyes.

"I'm Catholic. You're Protestant."

"--and get back to the way things were."

"But you must see they can't Daniel. I'm Liberal. You're Republican."

"Well it's all come out then."

"Things can't go back to the way they were."

"I get it. I'm an American soldier who grew up in small backwater Indiana to be exactly what you despise."

"I didn't say that."

"Nothing's going to change any of that."

"Not even me?"

He snorted out a small burst of laughter, "Why should I have to change who I am?"

"Maybe we should wait a little longer to decide on things."

"What are you saying?"

"I mean a wedding? If there is to be one. We should take some time to."

"Ah," he said, "So it's off. At least for the moment? Should I just hop on the next plane home then? That's the way this works?"

"Daniel."

"Don't Daniel me. You've changed. Ever since the last few days in Paris. You've become a different you."

"Maybe you should go."

"If you knew. If we knew. Would we have ever come this far? But we did. I got on that plane to Zurich."

"Daniel, I think you need to leave, young man. The lady said you should go."

Daniel spun around. Mr. Kent stood with a cane in his hands and Mrs. Tabernathy was behind him. Whatever passion still burned inside him to make things right was doused there when he felt the crushing weight of their disapproval.

"I'll go get my things."

Just like that he was gone as if he had never come. I stood strong until the door had shut. Then, in a haze I made it out to where my mother sat drinking her tea with all the dignity she had ever summoned still intact.

I settled into the chair beside her with a straight back.

"It could have been worse. You could have married him before you found out that he came from a different place. I was hopeful though, but an American soldier, Cynthia? I had never expected."

She patted me on the shoulder.

"I'm glad that we could expose him for what he really was together. Fitzwilliam told me that you had accepted his invitation to the summer ball? It's only a few days away, so let's get you ready for your official return to society."

"I had told him I was thinking about it. I don't feel ready to."

"Go write him now. Cynthia. Please, darling. Come to your senses."

With a little more prodding, I got up and went to my father's study. After locking the door behind me, I fell into one of the old arm chairs and cried. I didn't realize how much hurt I had been holding in.

When I looked up, I saw something jutting out from beneath one of the old books.

I went to grab it. It was a picture of my father as a young man. He had that same fire in my Daniel's eyes that looked to steal his destiny from the cold hearts of men that would hold it away from him.

Maybe it would be better this way, I thought. I wouldn't stand in his way.

I wrote the letter to Fitzwilliam and another to Devlin.

An Angel on the River Thames
Chapter 8

"Is that it?" asked Allison.

"Looks like it," I said setting the letter down and concluding the tale of Daniel and Cynthia at least until I saw Daniel, in the flesh at a chipper 96, the next morning.

"He doesn't go after her?"

"I don't know. I guess not. I mean there is a lot of serious stuff between them."

"But they're in love daddy, duh." She crossed her arms and then sighed as she fell back onto her pillow, "Daddy? Tell Mr. Daniel he has some splainin to do."

"Okay, sweetie. I'll tell Mr. Daniel he has some splainin to do."

"He has some splainin to do." She settled in under the covers and yawned, "I think it was a little anti-climactic. Not happy at all."

"Are only happy endings the climactic ones?"

She nodded, "Make up a happy ending."

"It doesn't work like that sweetheart." I kissed her on the forehead.

"I can't go to sleep without a happy ending!"

"Okay, okay. I'll think of something," I said and put the letter on the bedside table.

"What's that?"

"What?"

I looked at where she pointed. Another letter had been tucked inside protective plastic. Heavily damaged and misshapen from water or something, the letter was postmarked from New York to Indiana in August of that same summer.

Dear Mary...

* * *

I walked along the south banks of the Thames from Waterloo with my hands stuffed into my lightest jacket. The cold breeze snuck in through the space between it and my neck. I would've looked for some warm and quiet place to sit, but I wanted to be alone.

It's only when you really get to your lowest point in a while that you start to look back on your choices and ask the question what if.

I continued on down the river passing all the bright little holes in the wall. Happy sounds became foreboding and mysterious. My thin wallet grew heavy and uncomfortable chafing against my armpit through my breast pocket. My stomach stung in its emptiness, but the thought of food or specifically eating made my entire torso heave.

We had suddenly had it so good that I had forgotten what it meant to struggle and being reminded of the struggle angered me. It angered me more than anything else, because it felt as if something I had won fairly was taken from me.

It embarrassed me too. I had overcome so many challenges before. How could I have forgotten that things weren't supposed to be easy?

Anger buried inside deep and red like scarlet blood drenched across a field or the inside of an airplane. My anger roared and surged in me. Rage upon rage upon rage and nothing to quiet it but the cold wind off the river.

The anger bottomed out leaving me once again empty in defeat. My stomach roared. This must be it. That feeling that Mickey searched for and had hoped for in this trip.

Ol' Mickey Riley. I hadn't thought of him or the Hearts Club in ages. It had become a strange and distant past that no longer felt like a part of reality or even part of the pathway here.

I just wanted to feel full again. Full of love, happiness and hope. I would fight for it. Harness my anger and fight. Fight. Fight! Like the war. Like the years before it and after all again here now waiting for the sword of sorrow.

But I had been bested. Beaten by my own beliefs. Betrayed. Deprived of my future by my past.

Something too good had happened. I remembered Cynthia's words, but if things go badly, there is a chance they may go good again.

I heard a solemn music over the river as I was finally passed Shakespeare's Theater heading away from Buckingham palace. It sounded as lost and lonely as I was and faintly like organ pipes, so I followed it.

There was a cathedral hidden off to my right. I knew about St. Paul's cathedral on the north side, but this one, Southwark, I read the sign, would satisfy.

The church was black in the fading evening light. I couldn't read the time on the unlit gold clock on the side of the tower, but candle light and music flooded through the dark, propped open double doors so I came in and took a seat in one of the middle pews.

A small procession stood at the front. It didn't look like a wedding, a funeral, or a baptism. I figured I had dropped in on choir practice since they were singing intermittently. They spoke in English, but the accent was so bad that at first I had trouble recognizing church from chair.

I set down the kneeling bench which gave a loud clank. The procession didn't acknowledge me. I let my face fall against my interlocked hands. I hadn't prayed since Boston before the official start of America's part in the war.

First, I apologized that it had been so long. Next, I apologized for having not found a church in New York. Then, I said a prayer for Mary and her husband. I spoke at length to the ghosts of Josh and Red.

I prayed I'd find cheap food and a cheap hotel, but for now I had stuffed my bags in a locker at Waterloo. I prayed that Waterloo and my bags would still be there when I came around for them.

Then I came at last to Cynthia. I wanted to say something quick and thoughtful, "Father, I apologize for sowing the seeds of discord. I promise forevermore to love thy neighbor even when he does not love thyself. If you give me another chance, I will prove to you that I can stay true to my father without sacrificing your trust."

After another song by the choir I got up and left the cathedral with my head held high again. Devlin had told me about a cheap bar north of London Bridge on the way toward Whitechapel. The Red Lion or something of the sort.

I crossed the bridge, glancing occasionally at the water and wondering if it was cold. The streets were long and wound around the hills. The houses were like thin rectangles stacked and stuffed together and rising up along the streets like crooked teeth.

There was a quiet bar in maroon lit by a series of candles along the window. I had to come back a little after I had passed it and check the sign closely.

There wasn't a single red thing in the Red Lion apart from a few of the customers. There was something on a sign about rival soccer teams, but it wasn't easy to read in the dim candle light.

I settled in at the bar and ordered a liter of a local beer. It tasted like piss, but the large glass mug looked like it was full of bubbling gold. A girl at the end gave me a smile. I smiled back. A hand fell on my shoulder.

"I thought I'd find you here."

"Devlin?" I looked up from the half-empty beer and nodded, "What are you doing here?"

"It's my bar. At least I told you about it."

"Sure, that's right. Could I get you a drink?"

"Let's do that," Devlin said.

I ordered him a drink and we moved from the bar to one of the booths along the opposite wall.

"I apologize in advance, but this place doesn't seem to really fit you," I said.

"You mean it isn't as fancy as the Gold's uptight mansion paradise?"

"You could say that." I took a big gulp of the beer and it felt good to feel it sting the back of my throat. I felt my stomach start to fill and ordered another.

"It may come as a surprise, but not all of London looks like Mrs. Gold's vision of English finery."

"And the bar?"

"A place to listen to soccer games or football, if you're French enough, on Saturdays."

"Ah, fair enough."

We drank a little more chatting about the town until I asked him what he had come in for if it wasn't a Saturday.

"I wanted to see you."

"Devlin, if it's about Cynthia, I think it is safe to say there's no coming back from the hole I've dug. I've done enough damage I think."

"Poppycock."

"If you knew what I said."

"Cynthia gave me a little bit of the detail. As I had mentioned, that's why I'm here."

"And you still sought me out?"

"Well, yes you didn't do anything in your favor, but wallowing in your disappointment isn't going to help win her back."

"Who says I want to?"

"In that case, I might as well go, shouldn't I?"

"Okay, don't."

He didn't move at all and he smiled. I did too for the first time in a couple days. He had caught me.

"You can either grow up or dwell on it."

"That's my line," I said.

"Was it? I seem to remember hearing it a few days ago. Ready to grow up then?"

"Sure thing. Just as soon as I finish this beer." I put it down. "And get another." I went to order a third while he lit up a cigarette and gave me one too.

I didn't feel like it though. My stomach wasn't in it, so he put it back in his case and smoked.

"What are you proposing?" I asked.

"There's a Summer Ball," he said.

"Classic. You English ever have any new ideas?"

"You can't take the English out of England."

"Fair, fair." I took another drink. "So, what is the plan? You give me a makeover, complete with wardrobe, and I go in your place?"

"Hah, it's a masquerade. You'll be my guest of honor."

"Great. Now we're in midcentury Italy. Come Mercutio, to arms." Glasses clinked, another swig.

"It's not like that."

"No?"

"I take a guest each time. They'll announce us as Devlin and guest when we come in."

"Will she know it's me?"

"I doubt it. I always have a new guest."

"So, how do we go about springing it on her?"

"There is an unmasking after the first dance."

"Then what's the point of the masks?"

He shrugged, "A little bit of fun."

"One last question before we get started on the plan."

"Yes?"

"What's in this for you?"

"Cynthia never looked as happy as she did when she spoke of you the first time, and she has never entertained a suitor for longer than a week. I care for my friend Daniel and that means getting you together."

"She cast me off Devlin. Not too kindly. I know that you're confident, but what makes you think this will work?"

"Women like to be surprised and pursued."

"Not always in my experience. Besides Cynthia is different. She sought me out."

"Cynthia is still a woman first. She may be a firecracker, but with her chivalry didn't die in 1898 and it wouldn't be a bad move to throw stones at her balcony."

"Ah and so yet another quote of mine comes back to haunt me." I finished the last of the third beer. "Well then, let's get started." My stomach rested full and satisfied. My mind turned in the perfect place between coherent and loose to try just about anything.

"Now that you're thoroughly smashed. I have one final question for you myself. Do you love her?"

"Yes."

* * *

"Devlin Twigsby, Lord of Cantackeray, and guest."

We bowed. Some of the crowd turned and glanced in our direction.

"Well this is slightly disappointing," Devlin said. "Only about half the guests have shown up. Usually I'm on the later side."

"You said that Cynthia likes to come early?"

"Yes, I'll quick scan the room for her and meet you over there by the drinks?"

"And you'll be able to tell her apart?" I glanced at the array of masks much like my own. I nervously lifted it to speak even though Devlin repeatedly told me not to.

"Yes, she always wears this red one with a gold lacing along the sides almost like a pillow. It doesn't look as strange as it sounds. Meet you by the drinks then?"

I nodded.

"They have an excellent Lillet Blanc. Grab one for the both of us."

I found my way to the bar and leaned against it.

"Lillet Blanc, please?"

"Would you like the Kino or the House?"

"There is a house Lillet?"

"Yes, in fact, I think it rivals the Kino. Bests it even. If you'd like to give it a taste."

"Fine, I'll try it. Give me two please. I have a second joining me at the bar in, ah, speak of the devil."

Devlin approached with a distraught look.

"She's not here."

"Does that mean she's not coming?"

"It bodes ill."

"What should I be worried about? Her co--."

"Fitzwilliam Lucas, Earl of Southampton and guest, Cynthia Gold."

"--ming with another..." My sentence hung there suspended and Devlin gave me a right you are look. I shot him back a what do we do now, but he froze, caught off-guard. The man with the plan and the answers stood stuck in place.

"Say something."

"I'm thinking." The wheels began to turn and the tight edges of his jaw began to loosen.

"Do something."

"This is unexpected. The first dance. We have to figure something out by then."

"Why?" I looked over and noticed that the band had finished setting up and the music was about to start.

"It's sometimes a tradition. Well often kept to ah, kiss after the first dance."

The first dance started.

"What are you doing?" He yelled after me.

"I'm not one to wait for failure to come to me."

I took a swig of the Lillet and put it down on one of the tables along the dance floor. I could see the red-gold streak of Cynthia as this Fitzwilliam man in white led her proudly onto the dance floor.

I had been tiptoeing through life. Restrained, constrained and letting in all the bull shit. I had acted for a lack of a better word in the manner that I should or could or had to and not standing up against the hypocrisy when it was suddenly in my face. Here was my line in the sand. Only I would leave it permanent like a handprint in cement.

The faceless crowd began to step aside like colorful mannequins set to mark my arrival. I pulled the mask off. They could feel the intensity and the heat spin off me as the music swiftened. Here was my moment to fight for the hand of the woman of my dreams.

We were no longer figurative dancers on the metaphoric stage that is life. We were brought together by circumstance and drifting closer together on the lacquered wood like marionettes twirling toward infinity.

For a brief moment as the last of the crowd danced away it reminded me not oddly of square dancing in the park for the Fourth of July back in Indiana. Only with billowing dresses made of silk and the velvet gloves of party goers who were afraid to touch the sun.

"Daniel?"

"Cynthia."

Gasps.

"I thought you'd gone."

"Wait a second. This is my girl."

"I've come to win you back."

"You peasant I just said that this is my girl. Stand off." Fitzwilliam took off his mask. More gasps.

"I'm not in the mood for your territorial game of who was here first. She's told me she loves me and I intend to marry her."

"I said stand off. You peasant, and if I have to I will trounce you. I'm the Duke of Southampton. My father is Sir Henry Lucas. I have to warn you he taught me everything he knows about clashing swords."

"Trounce me? Cynthia, what is this, man, saying?"

"A gentleman's duel, you uneducated American. Outside of London town where you can legally kill a man. I was the best marksman in my unit and the best boxer at Cambridge."

I clocked him in the jaw. The music stopped.

I thought about saying something about his incessant nagging and bragging, but I couldn't bring myself to do it. I socked him again. The music began again.

He stumbled backward into a table and picked up an umbrella. He circled it in the air as if it was a knife. I put up my fists and approached him.

"It's a leaded umbrella." He swung it out at me from a distance but I dodged.

"You think that a little shit like that's gonna stop an American major?"

"I was a Captain in the Royal Navy."

"So you kept my seat warm on the boat I took to Normandy?"

We scuffled. I wrestled the umbrella free and tossed it away. He went for a punch and I took him to the cleaners with a good hook and broke his nose.

Then this damn tune that ran on the radio during the breaks at the Hearts club about a boxing ring in midtown came to mind. There was this American duo going up against some foreign pair and they always said, "We Americans don't brag or boast but if we show up your toast."

I let up when he finally fell into a table. It was probably only five or six punches. I tried to count. I fought the urge to spit on his sad body and then I did.

To the fucking moon I did. You'd better believe it and I said, "I've had it with this hoddy toddy shit. You're so English it makes me sick."

I decided. I was done. I glanced at Cynthia and walked toward the door.

It was the first real fist fight that I had been in if you don't count that time in the mess when Josh punched Red and Red's elbow hit me in the face before Travis the kid from Lawrence, Kansas, trying to defend me accidentally hit Terry and all hell broke loose.

Or that time in Geneva before the end of the war. Boston before shipping out. Well, if you don't count the war in general, because there are probably a couple more that I am forgetting.

Then there were a couple after it sure and then that time in high school at the football game on Friday night when Freddy wanted Stacey but she had been talking to me. Never saw Stacey again. Never wanted to in the first place, but I beat him blue anyway.

Gasps.

I turned around. It had been too long to be that last line.

Fitzwilliam had pulled a pea shooter. Blood running down his chin.

"What are you going to do with that? Clog an artery?"

He shot it. My arm felt like I had been punched by a tiny person.

I kicked a chair into him and I heard a crack that sounded like one of the legs had broken.

I was faint and dizzy. My arm felt warm.

Devlin. I saw Devlin.

I had to sit down.

I tried to sit, but the chair was gone. I fell not softly onto my ass. Where did the chair go? In all my years flying bombing runs over Italy and all those other times, this is what gets me?

A pea shooter to the bicep of all places?

With a bullet smaller than a damn dime?

Another figure.

* * *

So, that is it. That was London for you. I had a lot to do in the city when we finally got back. I didn't mean to worry you, but with Mickey and the club. Luckily, I healed up quick. Only a couple days in the hospital in the end, but Cynthia, my God, she never left my side.

The real news again. We will be getting married in New York this September. We haven't decided yet on a Catholic minister or Protestant one, but we've narrowed down a location. You must attend. Enclosed is the check for the trip and you're booked to stay at the Waldorf-Astoria on Park. Love Daniel.

* * *

I looked up and took a breath. A wave of relief fell over me. They were back together. Then again, there was a reason that not much was known about Cynthia.

Allison snored softly and I couldn't help but smile at it. If only I could snore as sweetly or that she could snore that sweetly for the rest of her life.

I kissed her forehead and said, "If only you could be so lucky."

I grabbed another OJ. I made sure the dishes were in the dishwasher. I brushed my teeth in the master bedroom.

I found my way toward the bed and fell against the soft, cold pillow in the dark.

"Marcus?" Shawna asked the dark like she wasn't sure it was me, but probably more unsure if it was a good time to talk. A lurching feeling of doom, then she said, "I heard the story you read Allison."

"And?"

"I couldn't stop crying."

"It was touching wasn't it?"

"That's what you're going to be writing about? I thought you said Daniel Kennig, the singer."

"Yes, it's his last interview."

"It's so beautiful."

"I know."

She leaned over to kiss me. I could feel where her cheeks had gotten wet and then I kissed her back. Pretty soon the inhibitions slipped away and we cast the roadblock in our sex life into the past.

THE WINTER
Book II of II

Danny, explain
Chapter 1

I knocked on Daniel's apartment door. I couldn't wait to hear what he had to say about the whole thing.

"Marcus!" Daniel said, "Come in."

"How are you? Nice weather today."

"Yes, have a seat. I've been outside most of the morning."

"Thanks Dan." I took the seat impressed again by how sprite the old man was. "Here are the letters."

"Oh my, did you read them already? You can put those here on the table."

"I did. Quick read."

"Well then. I guess I've got a story to tell. That's why you're here, isn't it?"

"You do indeed, Mr. Kennig. I must say you've got me. I'm hooked. I thought the war hero turned singer was enough to whet the appetite, but I was wrong."

"Hardly a war hero."

"Come on. You came back in one piece. You fought over the course of the entire war. You," I trailed off when I realized then with the look on his face that you measured the strength of the battle by the silence of its victor.

"There's always more to any story."

"Yes, there is. And, you were about to tell me more about yours. You and Cynthia," I changed the subject and looked at the letters.

"Where do I begin?"

"You left off at the wedding in New York."

"Yes, that's right. I remember. You know I got these from my sister. She kept them all those years. Gave them to me for my fiftieth birthday I think. Could have been my sixitieth. Hard to believe she has been dead for almost twenty years. She would be I think 105 now. 85's not bad."

"Hmm."

"Okay, I can see I'm off topic, but you've forgotten the real reason you're here."

"What's that?"

"I'm not special. That's the crucial point. My story is no different than yours. That's why it matters to you. You hear the echoes of your own life in the rhythm of mine."

"You could say that," I said thinking of Shawna and Allison and even Phil, "but everything stood in the way of you two and you made it work."

"We all face challenges. Similar turning points in our lives where we can go this way or that. It's an important thing I learned from Cynthia. To care for each other despite our differences. Our differences made us whole."

"Did you convert to being a liberal for her?"

He laughed.

"No. Of course not. I've voted Republican every year except for one."

"I see," I scribbled something. "So, you got back to New York and how did Mickey react to the news that you were getting married that fall?"

"He was both happy for me and upset. He wanted so badly to see if a slip up in Europe would change my style."

"It didn't affect you then?"

"No, it didn't. I do have to say though Marcus that the winter trip with Lucille Long out to California ended up being exactly what I needed for my singing career. It was also the worst decision of my life."

"Worst decision of your life versus best decision for your singing career? Which was more important?" When he didn't answer right away I added, "I had forgotten almost all about it. It was barely mentioned."

"It's been awhile since I've read those letters I guess. Do you remember the reason for the trip?"

"Money?"

"Close enough," he said and stood up to head over to the liquor cabinet. "Want anything?"

"I'm just fine, thank you," I replied.

He grabbed a bottle of scotch.

"You know it was really always right there in front of me the whole time. I just wasn't paying attention."

"What was?"

"The answer. The truth. The direction I needed. The right questions to ask."

"You'll have to explain this one to me," I said.

"I am," he took a drink before sitting down again. "You see in the world and in all things we feel that there might be some sense of permanency. It's an illusion. Everything good comes to an end, but something good may come again."

"So are you saying you and Cynthia came to an end?"

"In a way." His eyes grew glossy and he paused. "There's a reason I've been waiting these 70 years to see her again."

I made another mental note to be careful when talking about Cynthia as I saw him look up toward the ceiling and then refocus on me with a sudden flash in his eyes bringing out the young man I had seen in war era photos.

* * *

We made love twice this morning. Once when I woke up, he grabbed and curled around me from behind in a half-sleeping embrace like a hibernating bear and a second time when he snuck into my shower with me.

There was nothing proper about it and though sometimes painful, Daniel was tender and patient. He curled around me and whispered into me. He rubbed my back and my legs. He kissed my eyelids, my lips, my cheeks, my chin, my neck.

My soldier. I had once thought of the war as so dark, mysterious and evil, but now I had my patriot burrowing his stubble into my skin like a baby porcupine. His arms were not muscular. His hands were not so rough, but I knew that he carried in his heart the burden of knowing what it was like to kill for God and Country.

Yes that was sometimes terrifying, but locked in this embrace with him pressing deeper inside me as if trying to reach into my soul, it made me feel protected and safe. I held onto his arms and leaned backward to taste his salty lips. I could feel his scars running along his chest and body.

My hero.

We rented bikes in Chelsea and rode up the Hudson River to the Cloisters. In the past year alone, they had shot two films up at the complex at the north edge of Manhattan, but neither Danny nor I had seen the movies or the spot yet.

After the long ride up the shore, we finally biked through the rolling hills of Fort Tryon Park between the colorful trees with their red and yellow leaves swirling through the air around us.

October in Manhattan.

The second most wonderful time of the year in the city, because my first winter the year before had been spectacular. The lights, the trees, the golden chandeliers. The carolers, mistletoe, and sleigh rides in the snow.

I couldn't wait to share these things with Daniel like undiscovered treasures set out amongst the city waiting for us to have our moments over the year and future years, so that we might one day relive them together.

We parked our bikes and exchanged the sun drenched sheen of a New York autumn for the hallowed stone of the Cloisters museum with its myriad ornaments of piety, grace, and the suffering of Jesus.

As we perused these images of faith, I reflected on us. There were certain things we hadn't yet agreed on. We would go to church but we weren't sure whether it would be Catholic or Protestant. The important thing was that we both believed in the power of our savior.

Our wedding ceremony in the end had been Protestant in exchange for baptizing our children Catholic, but I felt like Daniel took compromising as more of a loss than a mutual win and for the first time I found myself conflicted.

I tightened my grip on Daniel's hand and he squeezed back. We listened as guides raved about the beauty of the sculptures and described their history to tour groups filled with Midwesterners with long voweled accents.

Mother had sent her regards. She refused to acknowledge Daniel or a Protestant ceremony. She congratulated me, but it was clear that she thought the wedding was a sham and she continually made references to returning to London in a year or less.

She never thought much of New York and didn't understand why I wanted to live here. She hadn't been back to the States since my parents had toured the east coast while she was nine months pregnant, so that they could ensure that I had US citizenship.

When given the opportunity to spend the war in New York rather than London, she had refused outright. She only considered the war a terrible inconvenience brought on by the egos and cocks of ridiculous men.

In her mind and she was to some degree right it amounted to a few border shifts, six years of an inability to get anything foreign from any market including her favorite Belgian butter, and it made family vacations to the Alps impossible.

However, she was being helpful with the lawyers and the trust fund to an extent. A limited extent, but she was cooperating. The lawyers were making life difficult enough without her help.

Between London and New York, and their knowledge of the size of the estate, they made dealing with the paperwork a full time job plus half of another. If the world was ever run by lawyers, nothing ever would get done.

It was nice to have the distraction, because something troubled Danny and I didn't want to deal with it. The night before, he said he had met with Mickey about something that we needed to talk about, but he had stopped short of revealing what that something was.

Secrecy hung over Daniel like a fine layer of snow. At first I thought it was just because of the war, but it lingered even after you heard a story the first time through. As you pressed into it like dough, it took on new shapes, folds, and creases.

It became kind of like a strange game that he didn't seem to realize he played. When I asked about Geneva or Japan, things that he had mentioned in passing, he described them as diplomatic missions after the war to help set up US bases of operations in foreign locations.

No more. No less. That was that.

In some ways Daniel had been putting off this meeting with Mickey and going back to work. I wasn't sure why, because even now as we ducked away from the tour group and out onto a side balcony that had a breathtaking view of the New Jersey coast across the Hudson River, beneath his battle-hardened gaze the drumbeat of destiny pulled him forward and further from me even as we stood still.

What aren't you telling me, Mr. Kennig?

He turned and looked at me. The veil had dropped from his face and I wanted him to put it back up. The words were coming out too fast for me to think about what he meant or how he said them. Too fast for me to hear all of them after the first one as the blood pounded into my ear drums.

There are times when you can sit and write a diary entry about the way life has gone after the fact, but that's not how life happens. Life doesn't wait for you to think about it and then come back to decide. Life confronts you with itself whenever you become complacent reminding you of the sharpness of your knife or the dangers of a rose's thorn.

"I went to see Mickey last night," Daniel said, "because, to afford the trip to Europe, I traded some shows at the beginning of the summer for a tour over the course of the winter. It will be outside of New York. Around the States. The last destination. The big show in LA. Will have almost 1000 people in attendance.'

"It's too good an opportunity for me to pass up. For my singing career. I know that we have the money, but I want to contribute. I don't want you to have to do it all on your own. I didn't marry you for your money."

"Give me a second to think about it Daniel," I said at last and found my way to the stone railing to hold my balance.

"I know you wanted to spend the winter together in New York, but it will be this one tour and it is important to me. There will be other winters in New York."

"Yes, there will be," I said, but I wasn't convincing enough.

"We've gone out. We've had our fun. We're here at the Cloisters today and we've gone other places like the Botanical garden and the sailboat races."

He had enjoyed those, but now as he rattled off explanations and reasons to go on this tour, it seemed he regarded them as trivial distractions from the pursuit of his destiny.

I didn't want to be in his way. I didn't want him to resent me. It took me too long to think.

He stood there impatiently waiting for a response expecting me to understand, but I didn't understand. I didn't want him to go either way.

Down into madness or out into the world without me.

Later I could digest. Think clearly. But later was far from now. What to say now?

"Yes," There I said it. I looked up in time to see the relief in his eyes but for the first time the feeling didn't spread to me.

I said, "Go. If you don't, you'll regret it your entire life, but if you do and succeed, then we'll enjoy that success together." But even as I said it I felt a pang at the word success, because I had a feeling he would, and I knew that it would change things. One good thing can come along and throw your entire life into flux.

"I'll write."

"You better."

"I'll stop by Mickey's tonight to let him know that the deal is on."

"Why don't you call?"

"I can do that too, but we'll be leaving in about a month," he said.

"Then we'll make sure we send you off with as much fanfare as we can muster," I said and he blinked then smiled after a moment's hesitation.

"Can you promise one more thing?" I continued. He nodded and I wanted to tell him to remember me, but I suddenly felt like that would be impractical and fluffy so I said instead, "Please don't smoke any cigarettes while you're gone. I want you to sing your best."

"Cynthia, I haven't smoked since London, but yes, I can do that for you."

As a crisp wind whipped around the stone façade of the Cloisters, I realized that we stood on a stone wall together and I suddenly felt like a wife set to stand on the castle wall as her soldier takes off into the vast country to do battle with dragons and sorcerers.

I looked up to see him staring off over the river and he looked genuinely happy. That made me happy. The actual trip with him gone, I knew would make me sad, but thinking about him happy made me happy and I fought back a tear.

Then a cloud shifted and the shadow of the Cloister's roof behind us spread across the balcony until we were covered in the brief darkness. The world was suddenly cold.

He turned to me and held me close, but not quick enough. I saw a grim decisiveness flicker across his face. I couldn't shake it from my mind as we found our way through the gardens and then biked back down to Chelsea.

That night we made love again. This time and for the first time I wondered which was more important.

Me or his songs.

Don't forget about me Mr. Kennig when you're chasing your dream.

I thought it before I could stop myself, and I started to cry soft tears trying not to wake him as he snored into my bare back.

I didn't want him to leave me alone. I need you Daniel, I wanted to say. I want to be your dream, I should've said. I had hoped that I was your dream, but I could see the drumbeat in your eyes like a fire burning within your heart.

Lucille Long and an Appalachia Sunrise
Chapter 2

The old apartment looked the same as when I left it, but I came back a different kind of person. I had thought that this was the perfect place and that I may never leave, but it was only the perfect place for a certain time.

I had outgrown it. It looked small and smelled like an old baseball mitt. I ran my hand along the mantle of the unused fire pit.

We had moved in together, but we kept my apartment because I had paid for it for the year and because our temporary apartment was just a little too small for each of our summer and winter clothes together.

I picked up some old, dirty clothes, folded them, and dropped them onto the fold-out card table that had become my desk.

I saw the window to the fire escape and instinctively looked for the cartridge case of cigarettes until I found it next to a Lou Gehrig signed baseball on one of the sagging bookshelves.

I stuck it into the inner chest pocket of my jacket and then rummaged through the thin, wide closet with the wooden sliding door for what I had come for.

I uncovered my pair of black Italian-style half-heeled loafers from the back under a pile of ripped jeans. They were my best shoes.

Not the ones that I got for becoming a major and coming home from the war. These were the ones that I had always imagined would accompany me on the stage.

I let the ribbon loose and pulled them out of the good southern cotton bags. They were a little scuffed. Just the right amount to make me look like the tough New Yorker I was supposed to be when I arrived in Tennessee.

The real important thing was that my father had bought them for me. He had saved up for an entire year to pay $20 for them at a downtown Cincinnati cobbler that went defunct at the very end of the depression.

He wasn't always the best man especially to my mother, but he came through more than once in a while and even mother loved him more than life itself for a long time. One or two bad days didn't wash out all the good ones. Unfortunately, there was one really bad one and I joined the Air Force.

I opened the door to the hall and on second thought came back, grabbed the Lou Gehrig ball, stuffed it into my jacket pocket where I would tuck my hands against the cold. I took the cartridge case with the cigarettes out, looked at it and set it on the sill below the window. I locked the window and set a wood block into place and left the old apartment behind.

As my footsteps rang out on the hollow wooden stairs toward the street, the drumbeat began to ring in my ears. Cynthia didn't know how right she was when she said it, but there they were again.

Deep, forlorn bass drums slamming just behind my ears telling me that it was time. My time. This time I would roar like the lion I was.

Nothing would stand in my way. A dream that had been mine since ten years before the war had started. Before evil men turned good ones into puppets and then sicked them on us like well-trained dogs.

A part of me had hoped the decision had happened then. It hoped that God would have stopped my heart quick and easy with stray shrapnel, an exploded tank, or an early detonation. The other half hung onto hope through long, cold nights in Southern Italy that I'd get a chance to live the dream that my father had supported.

I got out of the cab. The city had passed while I was stuck in my own head thinking that I'd have to do something really good for the God that had helped me get this far.

I went through the studio until I found the stairs up to Mickey's office. I'd come here so many times, but the stairs looked strange and detached.

I felt a little like I was pushing my legs along on a path that I knew I wanted. This was me. This was my work. This was where I was supposed to be, but my body felt heavy and hard to move until I reached the top of the stairs and turned the door into Mickey's office.

He had lain out a putting green and was leaning back against the desk. Gordon had the putter and shanked the hit when he heard the door. Lucille sat on a set of short steel filing cabinets along the back wall with her arms folded and a distinctly bored look.

Her guard dropped as I entered and Gordon said, "You're late."

"Come now, you'll have him practically stuck to your side for a good three months in a few weeks. Don't rush into something you won't be able to get out of fast enough." Mickey laughed, but he had that 'you' look on his face like he was about to close the doors and give me a good chewing out.

"That's right. Only a few weeks to rehearse for my Lucille's shows and this guy waltzes in like he couldn't be bothered."

"You good kid?" Mickey asked. I had caught that Lucille was staring and had hidden my face from her view by looking off toward the window so that Gordon stood between us.

I nodded, "Yes."

"The song book is on the desk," Gordon said.

Mickey picked it up and tossed it at me, "You'll be rehearsing starting tomorrow morning here while the club is closed until you ship out."

"You've met Lucille," Gordon went to grab the golf ball and got back into position.

"Hiya," Lucille lifted herself off the cabinets and a subtle waft of perfume rose up and into the room, "were you in Europe, was it? Something's different about you."

"He's a married man now," chuckled Mickey, "gives us that deer in the headlights look until we settle in."

Lucille smiled politely and she and Gordon gave me compliments. She started asking more about Europe until Gordon got fed up missing his putts and told her he'd help her prepare to rehearse.

I watched her go. Her perfume trailed behind her and hung around the room.

"A piece of advice kid. I wasn't too happy when I heard it went well at first. I was hoping that you'd lose the good Midwestern boy a little bit and toughen up, but my damn, you do look different."

I laughed it off a bit to hide the thought that ran through my head when I thought about punching good, old Fitzwilliam and broke his nose. It may not have happened the way you wanted it, but I knew what lurked underneath the surface. I had lost a youthful sense of virility, but it had returned as a calmer confidence.

"Good, different. Like a glow about you. Halo like. Makes me want to go to your same church groups. Anyway. My piece of advice. You'll be on this tour for three months or so. Up to four. Don't forget the things that matter."

"I won't."

"I'm telling you. I haven't given you a whole lot of advice. I lied just then. I have. But, apart from the singing I haven't given you a whole lot of advice. Remain humble Danny boy, in your pursuit of the future."

* * *

Rehearsal after rehearsal. The days grew long and lasted into the night. I went home to Cynthia and she cuddled into my arms and asked me how it went.

Not good enough, I admitted, got to work harder tomorrow. Every day we returned. I memorized the lyrics. I memorized the moves and steps they wanted. We hit it all in time, but then Gordon came out yelling.

We didn't have the chemistry. Not enough oomph. It just wasn't there. So we went at it again and again and we all grew tired of each other and then familiar with each other so that it was strange to be in the room without anyone. This feeling would pass soon too though it helped that Lucille and her back up dancers were pleasing to look at.

Gordon never warmed to the performance, but he grew less cold and he kept muttering as long as we got better by LA.

This whole trip hung on Los Angeles.

That one show meant the whole tour.

At first he kept it to himself, but he realized we knew too soon enough and he started letting us in on his view of the way things stood.

If we went into Los Angeles like this, we'd never sing another song in public.

The days became so similar that they blended together and one day turned into a week and the week turned into three, and pretty soon near a bus lined up outside Penn Station Cynthia draped her arm on me asking me why I had to go and telling me that I should write.

I told her in my half-awake glaze that I was not content to rest on my laurels. I would not merely reap the benefits of what our life could afford. I wanted to participate in the building of a shared vision.

What I didn't say was that I was born wanting more. I may have saved the princess, but it wasn't enough. I wanted to bring the world to her feet.

She looked at me with a reverent gaze that made me feel undeserving. I needed to prove everything to her. I kissed her and she held on tight then I picked up the old, green duffel that had made it through seven years now and boarded Lucille's tour bus.

I saw Lucille back away from the window and act like she didn't notice me finding my way to the back where they had set aside a corner for me. We'd be sleeping in motels from here on out or the bus in rest stops off the highway if we didn't make it to a town in time.

The bus pulled away from Penn Station. I felt the icy, cold wind of the morning air on my face, settled back and closed my eyes.

We went down 34th until we hit the tunnel opposite the inbound traffic of an early morning weekday. I felt us head under the Hudson and emerge from the other side into Jersey. The traffic was fast going out of the city.

When we rose back up onto the highway going south, I snuck a look back at the city and saw the sky emblazoned pink, red, and orange by the rising sun like spilled paint.

I followed the pink glaze to the Empire State Building and it finally set in. It was just me now on the long road out. I had really left New York City behind, but no matter how badly my stomach felt at that moment, I couldn't turn back. This was my road and I had to walk it alone.

* * *

We drove into the thick trees and wide mountains of Pennsylvania toward Pittsburgh and Ohio. The vastness of the fading green world disappeared in the night, but you could feel the car wind its way through the places where hundreds had carved away stone during the New Deal.

I stared out the window at the dark silhouettes of pine trees and the last leaves of autumn against the oncoming sun until sleep came with the sudden jolt of waking up late in the afternoon.

I knew there were towns out there and lots of people, but I couldn't imagine where they were hidden in the trees. Then, we would break from between the woods and come out on a ridge to see a long valley filled with strong farm men and surrounded by the immense forest world.

It must be a lot like Switzerland in the summer I thought, but it was the fall and swaths of trees had been cut away for the telephone cables strung between these open low spaces. They rose up and down these hidden mountains like sections shaved from the fur of wooly buffalo huddled together against the cold night.

I watched it all like it was the first time that I had seen it. A new America spread out before me until we stopped at a rest stop outside of Pittsburgh.

I went out into this strange new world, with a sense of humility. I forced my head high by reminding myself to and found myself dropping 25 cents for a cup of coffee and finding a park bench to sit alone.

I wondered what Cynthia was doing now. I would have to write her a letter as soon as we got to Knoxville, I thought and sat there with my coffee which was almost as bad as the coffee in Switzerland sinking into myself.

"Hey dreamer boy," Gordon came over, "Can you look for Lucille? We are about to head out, and I can't find her."

"I think I saw her head over toward the ladies."

"She wasn't there. Do you mind checking over by those grills? You see where that family has set up for breakfast while I check again?"

"Sure thing," I said.

"Now," Gordon said.

I finished the coffee in one bitter gulp and walked over to the camp. I thought the smoke drifting up over it was from one of the grills lighting up, but it was Lucille sharing a lit cigarette with a teenage girl that didn't look much older than 14.

"Don't tell Gordon."

"Does Gordon know about this?" I asked at just about the same time.

"No. He thinks that I quit a couple years ago."

"You should," I said.

"Don't be a hypocritical ass. I smelled them on you the first night we met."

"I quit them."

"For how long?"

"Six months," I said and then counted and realized that I was right.

She gave the cigarette back.

"Come on kid," I said.

"I'm eighteen now," she said and gave me a scornful look before tucking her hands into her purse and pulling out a little bottle of mouthwash, a tube of hand lotion, and added a spritz of perfume.

"Let's not keep Gordon waiting," she said and I waited for a moment before following her back to the bus realizing that something had shifted in my chest when I had heard that she was eighteen. She looked like such a little girl, but she was only a year younger than my wife Cynthia.

The other girl looked at me with the cigarette in between her fingers and poised next to her lips waiting for me to say something. I turned and followed after the cigarette singer, Lucille Long.

The sun now stood before me and New York behind as I walked back to the dark, silver bus hidden by the high ridge across the highway from the setting sun.

Stars Shining on a Tennessee Dream
Chapter 3

We arrived in Knoxville the next morning just after dawn had cracked and the city was lit.

We parked at a motel, checked in, and then got directions to the site where we would be performing down past the university's main campus by a new downtown area that had been refurbished on the heels of an exposé earlier that year.

I put on a decent suit and pair of new shoes that I had bought along on the trip courtesy of Cynthia. We took a half-tour on-foot of the new downtown before we made it to a large, long single room bar, Hotel Lester, that looked like half an old bowling alley with a stage in the back, an open mic night sign above the door, and a shallow dip in the center with burgundy carpeting where a set of nice looking tables stood adorned.

A proper gentleman with a grizzled grey goatee and a full head of stark white hair, a pair of glasses, and flash bulb smile that he was as shy as knowing with, came out from the back and greeted us by the bar. He wore a crisp, tailored suit that made me feel underdressed and shoes so shiny that they looked less like polished leather and more like spit-shined black rubber.

"How do you do? I'm Jack Williams, proprietor of Hotel Lester. Gordon. Fiorlini?" He said the name slow, but he pronounced it perfectly. It made me feel like an ass for having thought he wouldn't.

"Yes," said Gordon, "Is there a spot we can put our things? For the stage."

"Up those stairs to the side of the stage and you'll find a little alcove. It's connected to the changing rooms I had mentioned."

"Larry, Mike, you want to grab those bags and start moving them. You got a place we can talk business without the others around?"

"Sure thing, follow me. Could I meet the singers quick? I just like to get a feel for what I'm paying for."

"Lucille?" Gordon said and he waved me over too. "Where's Lucille?"

"I'll find her," one of the technicians said.

"Jack Williams," the man said with the quick, burst of white teeth and held out his hand.

"Daniel Kennig." We shook. He had a strong grip. "It's a pleasure to come down here to sing."

"A pleasure to have you, my boy, and who is this fine young woman?" He asked. Lucille had entered.

"Lucille Long, Jack Williams," Gordon said and then we watched Jack give us the lovely privilege to witness the mastery of a southern gentleman.

Gordon worked Jack back and into his office to talk business leaving us to set up the stage. Jack mentioned the same hallway that he and Gordon disappeared down would have three changing rooms. One for me and Lucille and the back-up singers would have to share one.

With Gordon and Jack gone, the crew, including me and Lucille, got to work preparing to rehearse a couple times before the show that night. Without goading or discussion, everyone formed a bubble around me like touching or talking to me would kill them and an old lurking, poisonous thought eased into my mind.

What the hell am I doing here?

No one seemed to mind if I slipped out the back and disappeared into the morning. It felt like only Lucille and Gordon acknowledged that I had come along on the trip, so after finishing what I knew I could prep and being ignored by the guys setting up the sound, I took a seat at the bar and got the bartender's attention.

"You got any good Bourbon down here?" I asked eyeing the whiskey display behind the counter.

"No sir," the boy said, "That's Kentucky that's got that. This is good Tennessee Whiskey."

"What's the difference?"

"To be honest, not much, but we prefer not to have any French tint to the name around her in our middle state. No disrespect to the French. They helped make our great country, but we got a lot of pride in Tennessee. You seen the new downtown?"

"Yep I did," I nodded, "Could I get a smoky one?"

"You sure. You look like a big city boy. Might not be your thing."

"I grew up just east of Cincinnati."

"All right, sir," he said. "Want it straight or with this new stuff that just came out."

"Straight."

"Good man. Coming up."

He put it in front of me. I looked over at Lucille and put the short glass of straight whiskey to my lips before scanning the room. She was busy with the backup singers who had a way of parting when I neared like a group of gazelles.

Gordon and Jack returned and we got to the rehearsal. Jack made a fuss but eventually Gordon convinced him to let us work in peace for the moment.

We went through a couple songs.

Being a little tipsy helped slacken my inhibitions, but the anger built in Gordon with each passing note.

The songs were smooth. The transitions were easy, but at the end of our third number, he stood up.

"Ahhh. Stop." He threw a clipboard against the bar. It snapped into two and one half skidded along the top and fell down onto the wood platform where the bartender had stood with a lonely crash.

Gordon tipped over a table and kicked a chair.

"You are so far from where it should be! You think that we will have a good show in LA with this crap?" He was talking to every one now, but I felt his glare shift on me. He jumped up onto the stage and looked me right in the face.

"Where is it? You have no passion. You're nothing like the singer we saw in New York. People want sexy. Can you give me sexy?" Split flew out and he spewed a couple more insults and then walked off like the Tasmanian devil leaving chairs and tables in his wake muttering LA.

I stood there with my voice caught in my throat. We had only six hours to figure it out before the first show, and I couldn't even get through three songs in the rehearsal without Gordon going off.

I felt nothing like the singer I had been in New York. I took my things, wiped the spit off my face, and went into my changing room. For the first time the crew looked at me, but it felt more like people watching a train crash happen before their eyes unable to stop it.

I thought about that last bit that Gordon had said before his words became an incomprehensible spew of garbage and profanity. Be sexy?

Mickey had mentioned that too. Sexy is the new classy, he had said.

I opened the changing room door. The light from the hallway stretched into the small square room with stark white walls and a mirror with lights on it that looked like it had been the property of a Louisiana showgirl.

A clean, crisp white envelope lay in the light on the desk. The letter from Cynthia.

Poison lurked in the shadows. I wondered if I had made a mistake as I sat in the chair and looked into the mirror at myself. I rubbed my hands over my face and saw how red and star-struck I looked with that faint red glow in my cheeks and water in my eyes.

I read the letter. It seemed mildly hurtful and subtly dismissive like my wants were subordinated to a whimsical male fantasy where something like fame could only happen to the better people.

Was I just chasing smoke or was something out here? She knew exactly how men worked of course whereas I had to give up on how women worked long ago.

I hadn't even been gone a week. There was so much that I wanted to achieve. I needed to climb my mountain. I wanted to be more than just her hero. Her white knight.

She could've come along too, but she had to deal with her money and mother and so stayed in New York. If that fell through, we needed me to do this.

"You'll do whatever it takes to make this the right choice, for the both of us." I mouthed the words quietly barely above a whisper, because I had heard footsteps in the hall.

The lights flipped on. In the mirror I could see a fine hourglass figure in the doorway. At first, my mind went to Cynthia, but then I realized it was Lucille.

She stood there in a low-cut shirt and a tight pair of pants like she had just gotten out of her traveling clothes and come here.

"How are you doing Danny?" she asked. I turned my chair all the way around and put my hands in my lap.

"What are you doing here Lucille?" I asked and glanced at the letter from Cynthia.

"You seemed distracted out there, but when I heard Gordon say we had no passion. I knew what I needed to do."

I breathed slowly trying not to give anything away. I could feel myself thicken in my pants. I wanted to kick her out and remove the temptation, but I risked revealing that her luscious youth swayed me.

"You see something that you like?" she said and glanced at the letter, "I can't believe you went and got married before I could tell you how I feel about you."

I said nothing.

"Don't you want to know?" She put a hand on my knee. I stood up and turned away.

"Save it for the stage Lucille."

She put a hand on my shoulder and I finally calmed my crotch using the anger in my heart. I turned and pointed at the door.

"Out please."

"I couldn't stop thinking about you Daniel since we met. I still can't. I had hoped I could."

"I said save it for the stage."

"I'll be waiting," she said, looking down once.

I closed the door after her and flipped off the lights so I could be alone in the dark.

I went into the restroom and turned on the light above the sink. It hung over me floating on the end of a chain. I splashed water on my face hoping to overcome the temptation that swelled in me and thinking of Cynthia, but as I thought of Cynthia, thoughts of Lucille barged in. I turned off the light before sitting in darkness thinking of a plan.

I put the light back on, wrote my response to Cynthia, and took out my daddy's shoes.

Tennessee Jack was a good looking man and he dressed well, but that wasn't me. The crowd wouldn't be coming to see a Tennessee want-to-be. I needed the rough, scuffed look that spoke Manhattan.

I needed sexy. They would pay to see the New York duet, Lucille Long and Danny K and I knew now how I'd give them a show that they wouldn't forget.

* * *

Murmurs spread through the crowd like a prairie fire when I got up to the stage in my daddy's old penny loafers and shrugged off part of my military gait for the edge of wild that I had earned in the Indiana foothills.

I didn't have to look toward Gordon to know he fumed or Jack to understand that he now regarded me even more like some pansy that grew out of Brooklyn like the rest of the male dancers in tights from Manhattan.

To prove them wrong, I'd have to prove myself wrong first and out of the corner of my eye I saw Lucille smile. I looked at her and thought of Cynthia. My heart felt warmer and her youthful, vibrant eyes sparked like I had said the magic word to open the magic door.

This was the moment when it could either go up or down. Where we either went forward or back. All the things in life led here like a mysterious and mischievous wheel of fortune that spun long ago and disguised its intentions until the last possible second, and when it finally all came together the puzzle pieces at the start seemed to fit better into the whole story than they had to just that part.

Get sexy, you said? I can get sexy. I would only have to flirt with the devil and disaster, but I knew at the time that nothing could come between Cynthia and I.

The song began. First the drums. The snare, the bass. And, then a trumpet followed by Lucille.

The talking quieted down with the sound of her voice and I advanced toward her.

Then it was my turn and I gave them everything they needed and more.

I used my hands and arms. I looked them in the eyes. I looked Lucille in the eyes, and I told her as if I was speaking to Cynthia about how much I loved her.

I stole a glance at the crowd and saw jaws dropped with happy eyes.

There was a massive round of applause after the first number and the second song began. We performed well into the night to choruses of encore, encore.

Some customers slipped out, but a strong core remained, and we continued on getting closer and closer. Our hands touched, our hips almost did. We leaned nearer to each other, and then it was done.

I bowed to the audience and went straight for my changing room. Lucille saw me duck away, but when she got to my door, I had already locked it and slouched into the corner with Cynthia's letter in my hands.

She called my name, but I didn't answer. She said something quietly but I couldn't hear.

A few minutes passed and then there was more knocking.

"I said come back later."

"Danny?" asked Gordon, "It's me. You got a moment to talk?"

I hopped up and opened the door, "Gordon? Do you need something?"

"Only to congratulate you kid. My God I didn't think you had it in you after these rehearsals. You looked like a different singer than the one I met in New York, but you really showed you might have it tonight.'

'I'm impressed. It's not quite as powerful as it can be, but Mickey was right about you. You're a hard worker, no doubt. You've got a real shot. We'll work on it some more on the way to LA, but I just want you to know that I kissed the tables on my way in here. You done good Danny."

"Thank you," I said and took a seat in the chair while he heaped more praise on me and talked about LA. My mind returned to the letter that I had already posted to Cynthia. I couldn't go back and change the words, but I could definitely write a better letter from the next location.

"Where did that come from?"

"I don't know," I lied, "Maybe I had it in me the whole time." I blushed. He took it as a sign of embarrassment, but I knew it was because of Lucille coming to the room earlier in practically a bathing suit.

"All right then. Don't tell me," he said, "It's probably better that way. Anyway, 7 more cities. The last one in LA. I know I've said it a lot, but get ready because that one is your shot. If you can bottle up what you had out there tonight. It's going to be good. A couple more nights here and then we're heading up to Detroit. Get some sleep."

I sunk into my seat and thought to myself. There was too much on my mind to sleep at this time. I didn't want to say sleep when I'm dead, because I didn't want to hurry the inevitable.

LA couldn't come soon enough. Gordon was right. We had a bottle of something good on our hands and it could mean a lot to everyone involved even Lucille. The crushing weight of the crew's expectations settled easily onto my shoulders. I sung for more than myself out there. I sang for us.

The Beautiful and the Young
Chapter 4

I finished singing Dream a little dream of me to this crowd in St. Louis and it clicked right then when they stood to clap their hands. I wasn't an upstart any longer. I had been here before. I knew what to do.

I bowed.

"Another one then?" I winked at an old lady in the front row who nearly fainted, "Just kidding. I know you've heard enough of me up here."

"One more. Encore." They yelled.

"Lucille?"

"Danny I do sure think we can sing another song for the good people of St. Louis."

She did that stupid accent in every town we'd been in south of the Ohio River. When we went to Detroit and Chicago, she called them fine gentlemen, but I knew that it was me that they were coming to see.

My people.

These were the same people that I had grown up around. We shared that kindred spirit together. I belonged out here in a way that I didn't touch the fabric of New York.

We sang another one.

We bowed and took our exit.

I made my way quickly to my room to escape Lucille and barricade myself in solitude when Gordon grabbed my arm and pulled me toward a side bar they had in the back for the performers.

"Kid, I got to tell you. You're money," he got me into a seat then took a long drink and wiped sweat away from his brow. "Pure gold out there." He fumbled with a cigarette.

"Thanks," I said and looked back at the hallway wondering which way Lucille went. I thought I saw her go into her dressing room. I didn't know how long I had before she figured out that I hadn't gotten to mine.

"We will be doing an extra show in Memphis, then next up is New Orleans," he said and took a seat next to me with an exhausted sigh.

"Back in Tennessee," I said.

"What was that?"

"Never mind."

"I've been thinking," he said and he leaned in and pulled me close, "So, we've had an extra show now with Nashville and then Memphis coming up. You've got this trip on the ropes. You're a professional kid. You're a hot ticket. You got the makings of being a real somebody."

"You got something on your mind?" I said and pushed his hand off my knee, "Say it."

He turned toward the bar and tucked his shoulder in as if we were conspiring to burn the place down, "What do you think of leaving Mickey and New York behind and doing this again with Lucille and I?"

"I'll have to think it over, I think."

"You think you'll think? No one gets paid to think in this business. No one gets paid to think." He put the cigarette between his lips, took a long drag, and eyed me.

"I've got to," I said and left it at that. I dodged his hand sweeping for my shoulder, ducked out the door, and bee-lined for my dressing room.

"Don't forget Danny, LA's got a chance to launch your career kid. Keep your head in the game."

I felt a sharp pang in my heart. I didn't want to think at this moment, so I didn't. I let the world form its shapes in somehow coherent colors and then strip them from me quickly when I opened the sanctuary door to find.

Lucille naked.

Eighteen year old Lucille.

Laying there in lace lingerie and black stilettos.

She stretched her long legs up toward the ceiling. The sweaty skin on her thighs shined in the lights strewn around the square showbiz makeup mirror.

My heart thumped.

I felt myself harden.

I couldn't hide it.

I couldn't stop it, but my head felt like a sharpened spear had been thrust into the forward half.

I stepped back.

She got down from the table and turned around.

I put my hand on the door.

She peeled her panties to the side and just before any of her womanhood was revealed.

I closed it.

Where was a cigarette when you needed one, I thought to myself.

Don't forget LA.

What was I supposed to do?

They didn't make guidebooks for that moment when you've gone too far down the wrong pathway on the long road of life, but I still felt like I should've seen it coming. All the familiar signs were there. I'd come down a well-traveled road to find the same sin I'd seen before.

I slunk against the wall and then found my way out the kitchen exit toward an alley out the back of the bar. Two lovers stood kissing out by the street.

My presence scared them off and I kicked an old tin can then picked it up and tossed it in a bin. I stuffed my hands into my pockets whistling to myself as I walked along the lonely street.

I'd write Cynthia a letter. See what she would have to say about what to do. I wouldn't give her the full detail of the thing, because there was no telling what she'd say or do, but I'd give her my thoughts on the plan.

I couldn't say that there was a situation. That would be ridiculous. I'd have to skirt around some things.

There was a soft, chilly drizzle in the air that hung like a thin fog. I looked up to see Christmas lights on the lamps that lined the street. Life had hit fast forward. I'd already been gone more than a month.

We had driven through Indiana on the way to Detroit, but we had bypassed my hometown by miles when we went by way of Louisville instead of up toward Cincinnati.

I sat on a park bench.

There were a lot of men that wouldn't have walked out of that room, but then again I wasn't a lot of men. I looked at the ring on my finger and thought about it some more.

There were only four planned shows left.

New Orleans.

Dallas.

Vegas.

And then the big one. LA. Los Angeles.

California.

I needed that one.

It was the whole reason in the end for keeping the trip.

I wondered how Cynthia was handling her mother and the lawyers in New York.

I hoped for some reason that it'd still be going on when I got back. If there was something that I could help with though I'm sure she would've mentioned it in the letter I got from her when I had arrived in St. Louis.

It's just on stage. It's not real.

I'd have to see what she'd say.

Another month of the trip.

I'd be back before Valentine's day.

I'd buy her a dozen yellow roses at the flower shop on our block. The one with the $5 orchids. Not the $30 place that sold the same ones.

I missed New York suddenly there in that moment. Just for the ridiculousness of the whole charade. We were all cutting deals with each other to help us feel like we evened it out at the end of the month.

A billboard became visible across the street. I couldn't see the brand name, but it said, "All we really needed was our little slice of heaven and of cherry pie."

Amen, America.

Amen.

* * *

We did the show in Memphis. It went all right, but I wasn't myself. Of course I got back in the bus with my eyes straight forward and my lips sealed tight.

Everyone danced and laughed. They're voices carried over the sound of the bus against the road. I couldn't help but laugh and smile, but there was a new kind of bite to it like the end of Of Mice and Men.

I looked out at the brownish-green hills stretching into the distance and dead corn fields that gradually changed to green and alfalfa and then cotton split by a thousand little rivers and tributaries to the great Mississippi until we found our way into the vivid green lowlands of good old Louisiana. The trees stood dressed in shawls made of creepers.

And then the New Orleans skyline snuck out from under that grey horizon line of the ocean and we had our next destination before us.

The routine remained the same.

Hotel.

Bar.

Rehearse.

Sing.

I picked up my mail at the hotel when we stopped there after the long trip and sure enough, there it was at the top. A letter from Cynthia.

I hadn't doubted that she'd write a response for a second, but I was cautiously optimistic about the contents. I needed a little bit of wisdom.

I wanted something that told me to gut it out and stay on the path even if the path sometimes betrayed me and every sign pointed away from my dream. Cynthia always had something deep and profound to say.

I guess I had expected too much, because now she just seemed jealous and spiteful. *She says I have been sounding dark, different, diffident?*

I put the letter down on the desk and ran my hands across my lips. My sight narrowed to black tunnels as I realized the sudden truth of the matter.

Why couldn't I just be excited about something for once? Why was it that every time that I was excited, it must be that I was in love with a girl? If I was focused on work, then I must be dark.

She just wants to make sure that I am happy? Why can't I just be motivated and passionate?

I decided to write her back that I would stay and everything was great and fine. I was wrong to have brought up that there might be reason to come home. Other than the whole thing with Lucille, things were actually going well. Lucille was just too young to understand.

It wasn't a bold-faced lie.

I was chasing my dream. Except for one day, the trip had been wonderful. Sure there were cracks, but this was the best thing to ever happen to my career.

She hadn't been here. Who did she think she was telling me that I am angry and upset?

Well my wife, but that's beside the point. The point is things weren't quite perfect, but good enough. I'd write her that they were good.

It was a small lie, but I still hated how true her questions were.

How does this get me closer to my dream?

It is my dream.

But is it? Aren't I your dream?

Yes.

I wanted to settle back into the moment before this one when I hadn't read her letter.

I wanted to live in my own reality where everything was as it should be and everything had its proper place in the order of things, but with an astute glance she had utterly and completely shattered that fiction.

I wondered then if that's why my father always told my mother that she better shut it if she knew what was good for her and always before she spoke.

Times were a changing and for the better. Cynthia was right of course, but this was my dream.

There was a knock at the door.

This meant show-time.

I got up and went out onto one of those balconies that all second floor motel rooms exit onto.

There was the same sun.

There were the same clouds.

The black asphalt shimmered in that same sun.

I held the grip on the iron white-washed railings as I eased myself down and onto the bus to the bar on Bourbon Street where we'd do a little jig and finish our gig.

I was just like any mechanic going to the machine shop. I was a teacher on the way to the classroom. Mechanical, robotic. One more show and then another.

A passenger in my own body.

A feeling that you'd get used to when the things you love disappoint you and the love you feel curls in black arms around your organs and twists.

Gradually the feeling receded and a new vibrant world stretched and shook into place like a hallucination. Everything sharpened and stood out like colored paper cut-outs in a 3D children's book full of fun shapes.

We rehearsed and then sang one of our best shows. Afterward, I found my way to the street and bummed a cigarette off of a guy with a tattoo the size of my face running around his bicep.

"Navy?" I asked.

He nodded.

"Air Force," I tapped my chest.

We shared comradery and rivalry together in a kinship only available to men of the American Armed Forces.

No sooner had I put the cigarette to my lips than a sweet, young, tiny thing appeared out of the card-board cut-out bar that sat on the wide, hot stinking street where the hookers strut in the open.

"Danny."

"Oh, Eliza, it's you."

"Who did you expect?"

I smoked my cigarette and stared down the little Bourbon street sitting alone in the great big world under the great big sun.

"Do you want to come celebrate with us?"

"Celebrate," I said.

"Yeah."

"You sure?" I puffed up a fine ball of grey smoke into the air and then looked at the fire glowing lazily on the cigarette's thin flute tip.

"It's New Year's Eve Danny. You were all alone on Christmas."

Any other day and any other me might have said no, but I was feeling like I had made enough of the right decisions lately and gone and made things easy on myself again.

I could take a play off or two.

"All right, I'll come."

I didn't need to have my guard up for tonight.

"We are headed to a bar a couple streets down. This street is over-priced and too expensive for what you get," she explained.

A small group had gathered at the front of the bar.

"The others are already at the next place," some guy said.

"How do you know?"

"They've gone ahead."

"Well, how do you know they got there?"

"I just do. You'll see."

"We'll see."

I walked along with my hands in my pockets feeling like I was on a relaxing summer stroll down a beach with some good old pals even though I'd met them this past November.

We disappeared from this sunny world with its strange shapes and fell into a dark, dim den where the sun in the windows looked like a yellow sheet.

Beers were passed around.

Some Bourbon and coke.

I drank a couple down and I still hadn't seen her, but I knew I had to keep control of my liquor.

Partly because I didn't know what I would do drunk.

The afternoon darkened through the door and in came some more to join our early evening soiree. Everything glowed into a soft, easy haze, and I relaxed into conversation with some of the crew.

"Five shots for five shows!"

"Come on Danny!"

We grabbed one each.

I drank.

Tequila.

The next one came and then the next and the next and the final one.

Whoa. I swooned.

I didn't know what I said and what others said or that I thought they said.

I regained control. I stood up straight.

I saw Lucy out of the corner of my eye.

Then she was in front of me.

She had on a thin smile.

Click.

The lights went out.

I was still standing up straight. My eyes worked. My hands and feet did too.

But Danny didn't have control anymore. The little man inside that wore the mask when the tape recorder stopped, had taken the ship.

* * *

"Lucille."

"I wish you wouldn't keep calling me that."

"Lucy makes you sound like a kid."

"My real name's not Lucille."

"I know, but I don't want to know." I said. "It looks like we've each got one on the other now."

"What do you mean?"

"I was smoking a cigarette."

"You want a cigarette?"

"Sure."

"Come on Danny let's go outside. I can't hear you."

We smoked in front of the bar and chatted about something that I was angry about.

The clock struck 12. We heard them yell Happy New Years from inside the bar.

She took my cigarette, pressed her body against mine, and took a hit before passing the smoke to me through my mouth. Her lips were soft and wet. Her tongue playful. I could feel her perky chest against my arms.

I could taste the tequila in my own spit.

"Are you done playing mouse to my cat?"

"No."

"I want you Danny."

"I know."

"I need you Danny."

"No, you don't."

"Don't you like what you see?"

"It's not about that."

"So you do?"

"I've got a wife."

"You've been complaining about her all night."

I smirked. That's what we had been talking about?

"I think I love you Danny."

She grabbed my hand and pressed it against her chest with a soft moan.

I shook my head, crushed the cigarette with my heel and walked away whistling Putting it on the Ritz.

* * *

After a day to rest our splitting headaches and hangovers, we came into Dallas for our show. They liked us so much that we had extra shows in Houston and Austin.

We passed forgotten towns, shanty towns, busy towns, and ranches that spread out over the wide world where the sun burned hot and the grass grew in different shades of green and winter brown.

We roared over the plains and through the big country with the open sky and nothing for miles. The bus pulled off Route 66 when we hit a small town. We joked with some locals who laughed at our wide-eyes and took us for milk-shakes and gasoline.

They told us the best way to drive around the curves that ran through this beautiful new part of

America that I had not ever imagined enjoying until it had appeared here before me and touched me like some modern pilgrimage into and through the many hearts of my country.

A rain storm overtook us and turned miles of open plain into a dozen icy lakes in every direction, but the highway ran on into the flat and barren desert-like immensity that stood before us.

And then when it seemed like all the world was just blue sky and flat grey emptiness, a great wall rose out of it made of stone titans.

A thousand mountains stood as one up and into the clouds. Out and away from us for hours upon hours they watched as sentinels guarding God's kingdom.

We were a single, solitary caravan on a journey west asking for entrance into this strange world.

Then we were up spiraling roadways and cliff side roads with views of the flat land we had left behind.

Each breath and each glance of that world was beyond staring into any of those old paintings of the American frontier. It was here and before us. The grandiosity and majesty of the American wild humbled me as I witnessed the curve and the shape and understood what it said.

No man may live here.

This is nature's place.

Men may enter, but mere men must leave.

The slopes are too steep.

The greens too green.

The snow too cold and white.

The lakes filled with sulfur and emptied of life, but crystalline clear and embedded into the mountains between peaks frosted in glacier white.

Patriotic tears welled in my eyes. I had been angry and hurt in the last year, but I had not cried. There was no crying in America according to my father and his father before him.

Not for a man of America and so I tried not to, but a single tear burst from my hold and slid down my cheek. It fell onto the hot black leather of the bus seat and dissolved.

I counted it.

While I stared out at the country wishing that Cynthia were there with me, Lucille stared at me.

She contemplated our kiss. She dwelled on it. How good it tasted. How easy it had been. How experienced I was. Too short and quick. She needed another.

Her jealousy for what Cynthia had stolen out from beneath her mounted. In that moment when we had met in that Italian Restaurant on Manhattan, she had decided that I would be hers and she would be mine.

But, Cynthia had taken me from her. If she had known that was why I'd be going to Europe, she would have spoken up then, but Lucille didn't understand.

Cynthia and I had shared more than just a moment in the sun together. We had shared one spirit, one mind.

One soul.

* * *

I woke up with this same feeling like I had dreamed the future.

My stomach felt a little queasy, so I poured a tall glass of water.

I took light sips and waited to see if it would go away, but it didn't.

I went to the mail boxes and found a letter from Danny had come earlier that morning.

The beautiful white envelope had a stamp from the post office in New Orleans.

I kissed the little stork and ran my finger through the gap in the envelope to split it open.

The package ripped in my hands, but a neat little square of Danny's folded letter fell out and into my hands.

I read the letter. I could feel the pain and indecision in him through his words. He lied to me and to himself that everything was fine, but he couldn't see that the trip was changing him.

There were plenty of other ways that he could work on his singing, but he had been stubborn. At first, I had thought he wanted to get away from me.

I still partly did, but I knew better.

If Danny didn't want to, he wouldn't write.

But he did.

And he was putting on a face to keep up appearances like he always seemed to when things didn't go the way he thought that they should.

I put the letter on the table. I thought about it for a moment. After some serious but brief contemplation, I had come up with a plan.

I put on a coat.

I waved down a taxi.

"La Guardia please."

"Yes mam."

"Where are you planning to go?"

"We'll have to see."

I knew Danny needed me now more than ever. Call it women's intuition or some sacred bond. We had missed Christmas and New Year's together.

He must be hurting.

We got to the airport.

"Wait for me here, will you?"

"For you lady. Of course."

I ran out and negotiated at the counter for a next day ticket to Los Angeles.

Danny's final show.

The world came back to me after I walked back out into the cold. I clutched the ticket to my heart, because it was more important than my Tiffany engagement ring.

A light snow floated in the air. I pulled the edge of my white fur coat against my neck and nestled in against the slight wind.

My black heels clicked against the new, white cement and the idling gasoline rolled into the air.

I hope you're ready for me darling.

I can't wait to see you.

How Innocent is the Gilded Tongue?
Chapter 5

We were in Las Vegas. I watched Danny carefully. He lurked along the edges of the high stakes tables. I could tell that's what he wanted.

I knew that I could give it to him. I could give him everything that he dreamed of, but he wouldn't listen to me. I didn't know or care who Cynthia was.

I knew that I was right for Danny.

When we were on stage, we were electric. A perfect fit, but when the stage lights went off and the bar room glow returned he morphed into an entirely different animal.

I watched him play Black Jack tentatively and throw any of his winnings away on Roulette.

Ever since that night in New Orleans, he had looked happier than ever but further away from me. I knew that there had to be some way that I could catch his beautiful eyes and fasten them on me for good.

I had the plan all worked out.

I might have to sacrifice the Los Angeles show, but we'd had a good run.

One bad show wasn't going to stop us from storming the country together with our love.

I painted my lips red staring in the mirror.

"Lucille, we're on in 5."

I left a kiss smudge on the glass.

"You're going to kill it girl."

When I got in the hallway, Gordon approached me still in his successful showman daze. All the glory was getting to his head and it wasn't even his.

"This is our last night in Vegas, sweetheart. Let's give them one hell of a show."

"We always do," I smiled and pulled back the red curtain to enter from the right hand of the stage.

We'll give them one hell of a show, I thought as my eyes adjusted from the dark hallway to the bright lights that reflected up off the black sheen of the stage.

Danny put out his hand and said, "And here she is now, the star of the evening. Lucille Long."

The applause came loud at once. A standing ovation. At this point they knew who I was. Who we were. We had given them some of the best nights we had together on this trip.

* * *

Lucille came out from the behind the red curtain and I paused for a moment as she blinked.

The world went like whoosh.

She looked so much like Cynthia that I had to blink twice and check again.

No, Cynthia wasn't here, but she should be. That was her place there that this imposter was taking, but I could see the semblance of the spectacular in Miss Long.

Lucille daintily, faintly, weakly grabbed my hand and curtsied. Cynthia would have clasped onto me and made sure to never let go.

But she had let go.

Only to let me chase my dream.

Supportive.

She was my red butterfly.

Where was my red butterfly now, I wondered. Traveling happily down 5th avenue? Shopping at Sak's or Macy's? She wasn't the woman beside me, but I could imagine that she was for a few more nights and then I would be back in New York.

Hopefully, everything would be the exact same and it would be like I had never left.

I hoped that she was waiting for me. My 40 year old woman wife in the body of a 20 year old. This little girl would never survive a meeting with my tenderly rabid wolverine.

The songs began.

* * *

I saw the way that he looked at her.

I couldn't believe it.

He had traded me in for a younger version before 6 months had passed.

The songs began, but I could not hear anything over the sound of my ear drums thumping wildly.

Breath spewed from my nostrils like flames out of the side of a carriage split from hell.

I didn't know what I was supposed to do now.

He probably expected I wouldn't find out.

He probably hoped that he could come back to New York and tell me that marrying me had been a mistake.

A little time with all of his small town Protestants and he'd forget about his big city Catholic wife that had turned down so much of herself to be a part of his life.

Well, I didn't care if he was a war hero or a war lord, I'd show him some of my piece of mind.

I'd.

She kissed him.

Right here on the stage.

I couldn't believe it.

In front of every one.

He looked surprised, but he didn't push her away.

Well, now he has.

But, it was too late. I was already strutting up to the stage with my third drink in my hand.

* * *

What did you do?

I finally wrestled her away from me.

Lucille finally saw the real look in my eyes. The one that was meant for her, and her entire disposition wilted like a blooming flower that had been doused in methane.

There was a commotion in the crowd.

More talking. Gasps.

Cries.

I heard a familiar well-practiced walk. The clicking high heels like the bullets spitting out of a chain gun.

I turned to see Cynthia grabbing her stunning dress and running up the stairs at the front of the stage. A single bare shoulder.

Time stopped. My heart couldn't beat. My lungs couldn't breathe. I was caught up in something that was suddenly much bigger than I realized. We were taken somewhere together without knowing that we would be.

She tripped and I snapped back into reality. I went to grab her, but she had already righted herself and I went straight into a shower of whiskey sour.

"Who do you think you are Daniel Kennig?"

"Cynthia I--."

"My mother was right about you. You're a good for nothing Republican asshole. I should have known."

"Cynthia."

"Don't Cynthia me."

"I can explain this."

"Explain what?" Cynthia roared and turned. "Her?"

I looked to where she pointed at the tender girl looking at me with hopeful, awe-struck eyes.

"Look at her Cynthia. She's no idea what she's doing here."

What little spine that she had gathered in hope shattered and she fractured into the meek, retreating broken girl. A grey moon that had come in between the sun and I for but a moment. Her red lips looked strange on her. Too adult for her kid face like white paint on a Japanese whore.

"Cynthia?"

"I'm done Danny. You've failed me."

"I didn't do any-. Cynthia?"

She waved me off to cheers from the applause and disappeared out the thick steel door of the emergency exit.

I looked at the tables. At all the faces standing and staring expectantly. At that moment it set in. It wasn't the image that I wanted to project, but only when I saw it reflected back did I realize.

This had gone too far.

I made to go after her, but someone grabbed me.

Gordon?

"Where do you think you are going?"

I made to turn to go after my wife, but he tightened his grip on my arm.

"It's us or her. If you go, don't come back. LA could make you."

I relaxed my arm.

He slackened. His eyes lit up.

I broke his grip and pushed him back.

"You're fired."

I said nothing and went for the door.

"I'll get the courts involved. I'll sue your ass for all you have. I'll get all that you owe me and more."

"You'll sue me? For what's left. What is it three grand?" I took out my wallet. I counted out thirty fucking crisp, green unused hundreds and threw them into the fucking air at him. I watched them fall together in the air in a solemn arc and then spill onto the clean stage in the dimmed light like pathetic thin dominoes.

You know what, I thought as he stood there slack jawed.

I poured the rest of wallets contents onto the hard wood. Five grand total laying there and no one flinched.

"I'm going after my wife."

I turned my heel on it and went for the door.

There was one clap and another and then it grew to the loudest applause I had ever received. The heavy door closed behind me cutting it off.

There was a cold burst of wind. It tapered off as I got used to it, but a light drizzle hung in the air. I ran around the building. I found Cynthia near the valet.

She must have a driver.

"It's done Danny. I don't want to see you."

"Why won't you?"

"Go away," she turned and started to walk away.

"Cynthia," I grabbed her.

"Get your hands off me!"

"Cynthia. We need to talk."

"We don't need to do anything. I don't want anything to do with you!" She started and I wanted her to shut up. "My mother was right about you."

"I can explain--."

"Go away! I'll see you in New York Danny when you pick up your things."

"Will you just listen to me?" I asked, I pleaded, but she wouldn't stop. I curled my fist into a ball at my side and let my eyes fall on the pavement.

She kept going. She went after everything that made me, but she didn't let me have a turn.

I knew what I could do to shut her up. Just what my daddy had done all those years ago.

It had worked then. It would work now.

Instead I put my hands on the ground and kneeled to her like a subject placating before his queen.

"I love you."

"For God's sake Danny get up."

"I love you."

"Stand up. You're making a fool of yourself."

"I love you."

"Well, you should have thought about it before that." She pointed at the casino.

"I know."

"You--uggh."

"I'm going to leave it all behind for you."

"You don't have to do that."

"I know, but I will."

"Oh Danny. Why didn't you just trust me from the start?"

The car had come around and the driver was out rolling up his sleeves ready to knock some sense into me. The bouncer came around from the door.

"I thought I had to do it alone."

"You don't, but anyway it's too late now."

"It doesn't have to be."

"Don't you see Danny? It's always like this with you."

"What do you mean?"

"The secrecy, the lies. There is so much that you don't say. It's like sifting through a desert for sand with you. All the time."

"What do you want to know?"

"Everything."

"You really want to know everything?"

"Yes!"

"You really want to know that one night my dad got drunk, beat my mom, and she shot him in the night with his favorite gun? That she killed herself before going to prison and my twenty-seven year old sister couldn't take me in, so I signed up to fight for my country. Is that the type of secret you want to hear?" I was angry again, but I had reeled it in turning my voice into a silver scythe cutting through the dark.

I was hurt and biting, but strong and the truth felt vindicating. For us both.

"Yes," she cried.

"And, that when you worry about your mother loving you, I don't worry about my father loving me, but I see the cigarette burns on my arms and the scars on my chest where the belt wrapped around my back? You had it hard growing up in a home where money flowed easy? Is that what you want to know? That I think you have no idea what hard means?"

"Yes," she sobbed louder, "I want to know all of it."

"I'm sorry Cynthia. There are still more things that you can never know about me. Secrets that I shouldn't even know and will die with me. For my country. For my God. And for all the love that we share. To keep it safe."

She sobbed and said.

"I'll see you in New York Danny. I love you."

"I love you too Cynthia, but I can't let you go without me. Not tonight."

"It will be all right Danny. Just give me some time to think about it. About us. I love you too much Danny to see you live with this alone."

"Okay," I said, "Will you let me ride with you?"

The driver cleared his throat and I realized that we weren't completely alone, "I think it's best if you stay here son." There was the driver, the bouncer, me and her. The four of us in the cold Vegas night, and I took a deep breath mentally preparing for how I was going to kill them both and steal back my princess.

"I'm staying at the LA Chique."

"She's telling the truth son. Though I don't know why she should." The driver helped her into the car and then went around to the front.

"I'll be there tomorrow," I said standing over the doorway as she cracked the window open. The bouncer put his hand on my shoulder.

"Okay. We can enjoy the beach," she smiled and wiped the tears away from her eyes.

"Sounds wonderful."

The car lurched and pulled away from the curb and she waved from the window and then stared forward. I followed the car out a little way, but the bouncer held me back.

The car stopped at the exit from the hotel.

The driver looked back at me.

A glint of white light on the edge of the strip. It was the middle of the night.

I tried to wave at him to look, but there was the drizzle and it all happened so fast.

Screech.

Crash.

Metal on metal.

"Cynthia!" I yelled and shrugged off the bouncer.

Fwump.

The front of each car went up in flames.

I got to the car, and I could see her there in the flames. Blood everywhere, but her face untouched.

I tried to get the door open. The heat of the accident had jammed it shut.

The bouncer grabbed me and pulled me away.

"No!"

Boom.

We got out of the way just in time to avoid being burned or killed by the explosion.

The drunk that slammed into the side of their car would survive the crash, and say that he was just trying to follow the lights. I could only remember the fire as Cynthia's life disappeared into the night.

The audience that had seen me sing started to come out to see what had happened.

I was on my knees crying. Staring at the fire and screaming with the bouncers arms wrapped around me.

I should've been in that car. I said. We should have gone out together.

I tried to make another run for it, but the bouncer held me down. I cried into his shoulder and he patted my back. Hush, he said.

Red Morning
Chapter 6

I returned to New York with a whimper. My tail tucked between my legs trying desperately to keep my eyes set on the ground before me.

There was no time for soul searching in the few weeks after my last song. I had called Tom and gotten word to Cynthia's mom in England within a couple days.

Winifred Gold answered in a cold monotone as if she had already written off her daughter as dead. Oh, the one who had married that conservative American major? That one? Dead? She already was to me.

She arrived in New York shortly after I did.

We didn't talk.

We contacted each other through lawyers like a particularly nasty divorce. In this one I gave her all the trust money with no questions asked. The last thing I needed was more guilt resting on my shoulders.

There were some times that I felt like a stranger in my own skin. It had happened before. I would push my feet forward and the world all looked wrong.

This wasn't like that.

A switch had flipped.

A flip had switched.

We weren't in that old world that was supposed to look one way and had rules. We were in this mortal, human world governed by the one immortal rule where nothing was perfect.

With each bright thing comes the dark and all true light is born in the darkest black.

I had roared. I had raged. I had stood against the evil, the wind, the cries of the lost, but I had finally been brought down for good.

Tom had convinced me to seek out help at the church. The community convinced me that life was worth living, but I already knew that.

I started to ignore him as much as possible, because he looked at me like I was a different person. Solitude comforted me. It let me alone to decide my fate. However, I had agreed to one last lunch date with Tom before I left New York.

I would wait every day until the day that God would take me living the most God-like life I could, so that I would see my Cynthia again in heaven.

I worried that my past could haunt me, but it didn't. It disappeared from the view. The ghosts were gone. I would have to live a good life to see them again.

Forward was the only thing that mattered.

To the moment when the lights switched off and the sun rose again.

I looked at the cigarettes in my cartridge case. I had the date with Tom today. After continuous prodding, he had gotten me to agree to lunch.

I didn't want to go, but I owed a lot to him. If there was nothing else of the old me that I was anymore, I was still a man of my word and I gave him my word.

The twenty or so white, clean cigarettes sat in three pretty rows in my cartridge case looking like paper bullets. I glanced out at the city and over the thousand buildings with its million people.

Someone was planning to rob a bank today, and there was nothing that I could do to stop them.

But, I could change myself.

I poured the cigarettes out onto the snow-covered street three stories below.

I watched for a moment to make sure they didn't hit anyone and I went down the fire escape to the old apartment. I had moved back in.

Most of my stuff was still here and I had paid rent for the year. It was March now. The last month on my lease. All my money was gone, so I'd have to make a move or hitch hike back to Indiana.

Breaking the news to Mary had been the final straw. I had carried myself with all the dignity and strength until I had gotten on that long-distance phone call.

Tom rang the door and I met him there on the street. He looked good. Married now.

His cheeks were red. His stomach pushed against his jacket. His breath fogged up the diamond panes in the window and he waved with a jolly old smile.

"Danny!"

"Tom," I smirked at his giddiness. I knew it was a front to get me back into things, but then I guess that is what we both needed now.

"You ready for these Reubens?"

"Ready as I can be."

"Good enough. Want a smoke?"

I shook my head and glanced at the small mound of snow where the cigarettes I had poured from the roof were nestled in amongst the ice.

We chatted about the Yankees and the upcoming season. I laughed for once about something. It was strange to think that we were here again.

This place just east of Broadway at about 19th street with great Reubens, but I always ordered the pastrami with cheese. This time I didn't. I got a Reuben. Swiss cheese and all.

It was still here.

Life went on. New York didn't care. It also lets me be. That's what made it right for me in the end. I had gone and come back and needing to be let alone to my own devices without being given up to the wild.

We were still here.

"Thanks for coming this morning. I really appreciate it. You working so hard on me."

"You all right kid?"

I nodded and we started on our sandwiches sitting across from each other in the park.

"I'm worried about you. Sometimes you sound as if you're talking like it's the last time you'll see me."

"Could be." I shrugged. "I just have a new perspective on things."

"Whoo, Danny, I don't know what to say to you."

"You don't have to say anything."

"Stop it. You've got to stop being so dark."

"Listen. I'm tired of the irony and hyperbole. I'm tired of how pointless all these little stories are about small things. I'm tired of people telling me who I am even those who think they respect me. I'm tired of it all."

"You sure you're okay?"

"No, but I feel like this is the only way things can be. No more tiptoeing around things like Robin Hood. From now on I'll either roar like King Richard or die trying."

"Okay Dan." He grabbed his coffee and drank a large gulp. "You sure that you don't want to take me up on that drink? It's on me you know and it sounds like you need it."

He grinned at me and winked.

"Daniel Kennig?" A voice called from the street.

"Yeah?" I ran my hand through my hair. Snow drifted up through the air like snow bubbles and a man, about 40 years old, approached us from the north path trailing a black Labrador.

"Oscar Jones." He put his hand on his chest then tipped his brown fedora which matched his jacket.

"Nice to meet you."

"You don't remember me?"

I shook my head.

"We met last year at the Hearts Club after one of your shows." His breath grew in the air and combined with ours above our heads.

"It's been a long year," Tom said.

I nodded and closed my eyes swallowing the last of a bite of Reuben.

"Always is," said Oscar, "Anyway Daniel. What happened? I had heard you weren't headlining at the Hearts Club anymore. I had planned to stop by the club until I had heard."

"Won't be singing anymore. Going back to Indiana."

"When?"

"I only got a couple weeks left in New York Oscar."

"Don't do that."

"Not much choice left," I drank some coffee.

"I mean why? You had such an excellent voice when I first saw you. I had heard you were out or gone, but your voice sounds just fine."

"Excuse me, who are you?" Tom asked. "My name's Tom Granger, chief counsel for JP Morgan & Co."

"Oscar Jones, the it manager of the Stork Club. The place to be seen in Manhattan. You would have seen half our dinner crowd in Hollywood just last week."

"The Oscar Jones?" I said, "I do remember. Please accept my apologies. I haven't been myself lately."

"Perfectly understandable," Oscar said, "Anyway, you got time tomorrow? Why don't you come by the club?"

"I couldn't possibly."

"You will and I'll see to it," Tom said.

"I can't."

Oscar chuckled, "Why not?"

"I don't..." I began. Have it, I wanted to say, but it sounded stupid, so I stopped myself.

"This is your chance to roar," Tom slapped me in the arm.

"Sounds like I came at the perfect time. How can you roar if you're about to turn tail and run. Come by." Oscar scribbled notes on the back of an embossed personal card with a thick ballpoint pen and handed one to each of us, "Here. Tomorrow, take this to the bouncer at the door. You'll make sure he gets there?"

"You bet," Tom said. Oscar shook our hands and walked his perfectly behaved black lab off toward Broadway.

"This is your chance Danny," Tom said.

"To do what?"

"There you are?"

"What?"

"The Old Danny. Always need to be talked into doing a good thing when it comes along."

"Tom. You don't understand."

"Shut it Danny. I might be the only one in this park that does. You're too good to disappear from the world and hide away in Indiana. Didn't you just hear what Oscar Jones said?"

"But--"

"But nothing."

"You didn't even know who Oscar Jones was ten minutes ago."

"So what? I heard what he said and I'm not going to let my best friend be an idiot."

He had never called me his best friend before. It took me by surprise and I shut up.

"I'm going to stay overnight in your apartment to make sure you make this appointment and don't think for a second that I won't. Life gives us all bad breaks. I know that you'll never get over it. No one expects you to, but you need to live. You can't quit on me, because you can't. And you know that Cynthia would be upset at you if you did."

I reddened and sat up, but his stare was serious. He had played a new card. He would out stubborn me if he had to. I had to concede that he convinced me that singing for Oscar Jones was worth a try, but I waited a few extra seconds just to make sure he didn't think he had won that easily.

"Fine. Stay overnight. But I've got the bed."

"Good. I've been sleeping on the couch at home for a couple weeks anyway."

"What happened?"

"It's not important."

"Come on Tom."

"We can talk about it later tonight. It'll be like a school boy sleepover. Let's stop by my apartment, so that I can leave a note for my wife."

I put a hand on his shoulder knowing for the first time since the accident had happened a little over a month before that my friend had needed me as much as I needed him. He needed me in New York and he needed me to participate in life, because it was difficult for him too.

"What?"

"I'm here for you Tom."

One More Song Tonight
Chapter 7

Tom woke me up.

Shaved, showered, and dressed, he ushered me into the shower.

I lathered my badger hair brush in shave soap and wiped it over my cheeks and then shaved with my safety razor.

He joked that it was taking me awhile, and it was. He was excited. I realized that I should be excited too. This was exciting.

He had never been a part of a show or the behind the scenes part before, but I had and it hadn't been this 'little kid on Christmas' since the first time I sang a rehearsal at the Hearts Club and got lambasted by Mickey.

Tom took it to another level. He had one of those I know something you don't know smiles. I pomaded my hair and gave up trying to calm him down.

I locked the door behind us, we went out onto the street, and it set in.

I was back.

I tightened my scarf around my neck, buttoned up my jacket, and pulled on my gloves.

Tom grinned beside me on the street.

Life for a little while had felt like it was getting away from me. Time had started to speed up and run off without me, but everything looked normal again.

The street. The cars. The people.

I noticed the shine on the metal. I saw the array of colors on their scarves and hats and mittens. I watched their breath puff lazily into the air.

I could smell donuts baking down the street.

"Want to hail a cab?" Tom asked. "We've still got about an hour until Oscar wanted us there."

"Let's walk," I said.

We went west down Prince street to 6th avenue, the Avenue of the Americas, and then up 6th and north.

We took it to Houston and then made our way toward Bleecker until we hit 7th which we followed until we hit Christopher where we stopped at the Waverly Place corner and got a couple breakfast sausages in slaw and coffees.

We followed that back to 6th past the library and up to 14th where we went east until we got back to Union Square. Tom convinced me to walk up Broadway for a little while and we kept on it up until Madison Square.

As a light snow picked up and cut through the air like soft rain, I noticed for the first time the first signs of spring. Saplings and little tulips poked from the snow. Birds clumped and swung through the air.

The little shops on the street were painted in bright colors, and their display windows were filled with beautiful clothing and furniture. Pretty men laughed and pretty women played with their hair.

We chatted about it and the weather and how we looked forward to camping in the summer and enjoying Central Park in the spring. We cut through the park at Madison and west to Park which we took up to 40th street.

Grand Central blocked the street ahead of us, so we took the left and turned north at the main branch of the New York public library on 5th.

Tom got us another couple coffees from a hawker in the park and we walked one circle and then north on the west side of 5th avenue until we got to Rockefeller center.

We pointed out the flags and talked about having traveled and having wanted to travel together once upon a time. It seemed impossible at this point, but we shrugged and joked and then went north further until we had passed St. Patrick's Cathedral and I pushed a tear from my eye.

The Stork Club.

"We're a little late," I said having realized a little while ago that the trip had run closer to three hours.

"We needed the walk," said Tom, "Better here and ready than here early and not."

The handles on the interior doors were made of gold. The bouncer put a hand in front of us.

Tom fished out the embossed card and gave it to him. The bouncer buzzed the door said something to a woman named Paula and then shooed us in.

We came into a lounge that was furnished like an exceptionally inviting house.

Paula sat on a chaise with a strapless dress.

She smiled and took our names then disappeared to grab Oscar.

We waited for what felt like hours arguing about whether it was worth it to get that piss worthy coffee in Bryant Park. I argued that it always settled my nerves.

Oscar appeared, smiled, introduced a few of his assistants and then ushered us further inside the labyrinth.

We passed through the VIP room and went past the stage and then the kitchens until we got to a recording studio in the back with sound proofed walls.

"Some other clubs like to cut costs by auditioning out of Manhattan in old warehouses. I never liked that much. It doesn't seem to come through as good in those places."

Oscar described the walls and the process. He gave me a song and showed me how I'd sing along to a recorded band. I kept comparing everything to the way Mickey ran things for the Hearts in Brooklyn.

Everything that Oscar did he seemed to do it specifically to avoid being like Mickey.

"You've had the grand tour now. Are you set?"

I nodded.

"It's okay to be nervous. We'll do this five or six times if we have to."

"All right."

"We want to make sure we get you on track for at least one full song."

"I can do that."

"Grand. Find yourself a comfortable place to stand. We'll keep the water out of the room for now. Too much electrical equipment. If you need something wave at us through the glass. We won't be able to hear you when the door's closed."

"I got it."

"Okay."

"Where'd you get this song? I don't recognize it."

"We hire songwriters or are contacted by professionals who want their work used. This is a piece that we hope to roll out at the club in the next season."

"All right. I'm ready."

"Do you need to hear the tune?"

"Play the song with just the instruments once for me."

He played it and my heart started to thump to the beat. Tom smiled at me and gave me a thumbs up.

The drums began first to set the tempo.

The instruments followed.

I came in after a saxophone descended out according to the music. I sang the lyrics as they were written, but when it said she and you, Cynthia came to mind and I couldn't help the tears that sat on the edges of my eyes.

I held the last note until the last instrument ended and then the song stopped.

It might have been the last time I sang a song for anyone but it felt pretty good.

It was all for Cynthia in the end I guessed. I knew she had heard it somewhere.

I couldn't see them through the glass. When they had flipped on the lights, there was a strong glare.

I waved.

One of the assistants opened the door.

His cheeks were wet like he had splashed himself with water just then.

"Where's Tom?" I asked.

"He went to make a call to his wife."

"You look like you've been crying."

"I was."

"What's up? Something funny?"

Oscar shook his head.

"Danny, you have it."

"What do you mean?"

"I've never heard something so beautiful in my life."

"You're playing me."

"It was so painful, but strong," he said and then with a far off look said, "A lot happened this year." He didn't press any further. "You're hired. When can you start?"

"I'm leaving for Indiana in less tha--."

"No, you're not."

"I'd have to make twice what I did to stay here," I told him, "I had been getting my place for a discount."

"I'll pay you triple."

"What?"

"No, four times. Whatever you were making at the Hearts Club. I will pay you four times that."

I had to stop speaking and calculate what that was in my head. I was always halfway decent at mental math, but it took me some time to get back into it after a bit.

"Danny," Oscar grabbed me, "You have it. Don't you see? Don't you know what this means?"

I shook my head.

Brave Hearts in the Dark
Chapter 8

"And the rest as they say is history," Daniel
told me with a sheepish grin.

"So Oscar signed you on the spot. You were at
the Stork club for."

"Three weeks."

"And then you exploded."

"You could say that."

"You toured the country. You toured the world.
You had multiple gold albums and then one of the
first records marked platinum. I'm just listing the
easy ones. Exactly 60 years of stage time. You
performed at such venues as the Carnegie Hall,
Royal Albert, Vienna Musikverein and the
Philharmonie in Berlin where the Philharmonics
play. You even christened The House in Sydney.
While active your songs were some of the first LPs,

EPs, CDs, and among the first to be downloaded and streamed."

"Yep I did all that."

"You've sung at receptions for eleven presidents?"

"Thirteen if you count the USO show and I came out of retirement to sing one song for our previous president."

"Wow. What was it like to meet them? Many of whom you didn't vote for."

"They were all a little different. Passionate is probably the common denominator. Richard once walked across a beach in his wingtips. Press had a field day, but I liked that he had the guts."

"It must have been exciting, but lonely. You said if I remember correctly that you never dated."

"Never. You take the good and the bad with each decision. I never expected it to last as long as it did, but I was glad for every minute of it."

"And you've been waiting for Cynthia all this time?"

"Yep."

"Without a single photo to remember her by?"

"You grew up in a very different time than I did Marcus." He chuckled and got up to refill his glass.

"Yeah, meaning?"

"It was in those days, you see, that we didn't have phones or disposable cameras. We saw the world once. There were no second chances. I didn't even own a black and white camera until decades later, and it felt stupid and fake."

"How did you share the places you traveled to as a singer with your sister?"

"I grabbed postcards when I could to write letters. That was the thing."

"But, you're saying that I should still go to see the Rockies and the Great Plains. I've seen pictures. I've heard about them. I mean I know what they look like."

"Do you? I find that sentiment infuriating. Even my generation started to do it at one point."

"What's the difference?"

"I can't really describe it to you Marcus. The difference between a photo and reality, but when I close my eyes I can see that American wilderness still untouched. Vast, immense, powerful. I feel like that's why I got along so well with my fans all around the United States. I saw the world as if through their eyes."

"Of course it was also a different world then. It was safer to travel the States."

"Hah," he laughed, "That's a fearful man talking. There is nothing to fear from anyone in this great country. The Midwesterners and Southerners always seem to have a competition for who is the most welcoming and has the best barbecue."

"I'm black Daniel."

"You'll never know if you don't go."

"I don't think you understand."

"Do you have kids?"

"A daughter."

"What do you tell her? To believe in the good of humanity and stand up for herself and her classmates, or to run and hide in her room and avoid going outside to play."

I couldn't answer, because I knew that it was too often the latter. It was so easy to let educational video games take the place of games of hop-skotch and kick the can with the neighborhood kids.

There was always the risk that something bad could happen. She seemed to like them better too, but then I remembered the days that I ran through woods looking for sticks that looked like machine guns with my best friends and neighborhood kids. How we had learned to get along by working together.

"I was worried that that was the case."

"Well, you're not in my position."

"It may be strange to hear, but I was once in your daughter's position."

"That might be the one thing you've told me that I don't completely believe."

Daniel shrugged, swirled his brandy, drank, and then stared at the baseball on the mantle of the fireplace in his living room.

"All true strength is born through pain."

"I get that from your story, but I can't force anything on her."

"No and you shouldn't, but it takes a lot longer to live than it does to dream. You've got to start somewhere." Daniel sat down in his arm chair and looked at me with his soft unassuming gaze. "I could've done things differently Marcus, but I didn't. This is the way they turned out. I can't do anything about the past, but I can be hopeful for the future."

"All right Daniel. I'll work on it." The clock blared and I checked my phone. "Ooh shit. I am sorry to cut you off Daniel, but we are running short on time. I've got to pick my daughter up from school around 4. I'll have to take the LIRR out in about twenty minutes."

"That's fine. This is going to be a book right? When is the first draft due?"

"Not for another month. I'll be fine I think to get it done, but."

"If you have any questions, you know where to find me," he sipped the brandy, "I'm still here."

"Definitely will be in touch, but before I go, I'm looking for your final thoughts. A closing remark. If you were to describe it in a sentence, your experience. The stage. The love. Life with Cynthia Gold. All of it. What drove you. What was it all about in the end?"

"That's a lot of questions in one Marcus, but I've thought about it a lot. I'm 95 after all."

"Six."

"Yes, that's right. You see. Been planning this line for at least more than a year."

"You have thought about it then."

"I would say," he nodded, swallowed his spit, puffed up his chest looked me in the eyes and pointed straight at my heart. "I would say that brave hearts collided in the dark swirling together through mystical reverie and past pillars of catastrophe turning hope into reality until at last they became one. A singularity."

"That's good. It sounds like free verse."

"You got it?"

"Yes, I think so." I finished scribbling, "I'll have to steal that."

"I'm 96 Marcus. I don't care what you write. It's all behind me now."

* * *

Marcus took a little while to pack up his things and say goodbye. It was interesting officially calling the public life quits when I thought it had left me behind almost a decade beforehand when the song pipes stopped piping.

I walked him to the street where I had thrown my cigarettes all those years ago.

As we walked he said some more things, told me about his daughter. I listened, but my mind was somewhere else. I could certainly have done things differently, but long ago I had come to terms with the fact that I wouldn't have.

I'd do all the same things again. I would take the same good with the same bad, because you had to have the bad to have the good. It was the immortal rule. It was something that Cynthia had taught me long before I had figured out what she meant.

We waved goodbye.

Then, I climbed back up the stairs and settled back into my big old red armchair, took up my brandy, and drifted to the first thought that came to mind.

It came on soft and easy at first until it enveloped me in the moment and my vision became real.

It was a cold day.

That fifth of April.

I remember it like it was yesterday.

Made in the USA
Middletown, DE
06 April 2017